WILD SKIES

A Yeehaw Dragons Story

K.E.Andrews

For those who have always wanted to own a dragon.

Chapter 1
Bounty

The House whiskey of the Broken Claw Saloon said a lot about the establishment. Perched near the outskirts of the Melted Lands and the Alamedian territory of Lightspur, Dunesburg's saloon held its doors open to any wayward traveler needing a meal and a place to escape the heat. Its whiskey was unassuming but warm, with just enough burn to erase the dust of the road, and it didn't taste like regret the next morning. The dark amber liquor mixed well with the jaunty tune coming from the piano playing in the corner. The smokey taste matched the haze of pipe smoke filtering through beams of dingy sunlight.

Leaning against the bar, Dale Hartwell looked over the wanted poster next to his drink. A dark ring left by his glass stained the corner of the crumpled paper. The poster contained the vaguest descriptions, a rough sketch of a hooded figure with a featureless mask, and the name "Talon". The bandit had been haunting the railways for years, never really drawing Dale's attention. But it was the reward of eight hundred gold scales, dead or alive, that now enticed him—and anyone else hungry for coin.

Dale touched the pewter medallion hanging from his neck, his thumb moving over the raised lines of the twin pistols crossing a cactus blossom. *Eight hundred scales could buy a lotta supplies. And a lotta information...Might even be able to follow that lead in Edin "One-eyed" Sean told me about.* He licked whiskey from his lips. The cool alcohol burned his throat, washing down the salty, buttery taste of the aurochs steak he'd eaten.

"Need a top off?" the barkeep asked. Sweat glistened off his patchy, bald head. The pepper-gray mustache perched above his mouth like a caterpillar. His tweed vest had seen better days, the brown plaid faded by the years.

"Nah. This one's enough," Dale told him with a crooked grin and swirled the contents of his glass around.

"Thought ya were celebratin'."

"Still gotta be sober enough to ride. I'll take a bottle of Malistar and water for later, though."

Dale glanced past the barkeep. Above the shelves full of bottles hung a longhorn bison skull with a mageslinger spell circle drawn on its bleached forehead, its horns painted orange, blue, and yellow. It was a totem of good luck that toed the line between the Golden Flame-graced Alamedian territories and the wilderness of the Melted Lands.

The older man grabbed a large green bottle and a smaller brown one down, setting them down in front of Dale. "And what about him? He need a drink?" He peered over the bar.

Lying tied up and unconscious on the ground was a blond-haired man in a dusty coat. Blood specked his mustache, and a ripe shiner darkened his left eye. People stepped around him and otherwise ignored him. Dale nudged the man with his boot, but he didn't stir.

"Earl will be fine. I'm sure he'll get one once he's processed in the Rosewater Jail. He'll need it once the sleepdust wears off." *Maybe I used a bit too much on him...*

"What'd he do?" the barkeeper asked.

"Robbed a bank and shot the mayor of Greentayle. Been on the run for a few weeks 'til I caught him down in the Crimson Bluffs tryin' to stash his loot," Dale told him, arms folded across the top of the bar.

The barkeep's brow furrowed, and he filled two glasses with dark amber liquid. He slid them down the bar to another patron at the end. Droplets of liquid sloshed onto the worn wood, and he touched his thumb to the barbed ring on his pointer finger, drawing a bead of blood. He drew his finger in the air, creating a circle of magic runes that shimmered before shooting toward the droplets. As they hovered over the stain, it vanished, and the spell dissipated.

Might've been easier for him to wipe it down, but I guess he doesn't like stains. Dale looked at the stainless bar top. *Will say this is the cleanest bar in an outskirts saloon I've ever seen. Wonder if he can use his mageslingin' to make drinks...*

The man wiped his thumb off on a red handkerchief. "Greentayle is a fair piece from here. Why take him to Rosewater?"

"He's wanted there first for another robbery. Gotta drop him off there to collect the reward before Greentayle's sheriff pays him a visit. Seems like good ole Earl can't keep his fingers from bein' sticky. But people like him keep me in business."

The barkeeper grabbed another glass to fill with a bright green spirit. "Thinkin' 'bout huntin' down the Talon?"

"Wanted a challenge, y'know?" Dale replied. *Maybe Russel knows about Talon. If anyone would know somethin', he would.*

"Seen a lotta hunters and trained mageslingers come through, but it's a fool's quest, chasin' after a ghost like that. Few ever come back."

"Is that so? Maybe I'll get lucky this time."

The barkeeper frowned. "Pride like that is what gets folks killed."

"I'm just confident in my skills, sir." Dale smiled and folded the poster up, slipping it into the breast pocket of his vest. He rested his hand against the yellowed dragon horn revolver holstered at his side, the long stock brushing against his hip. The same design on his necklace was etched onto the cylinder. Its weight was a familiar comfort.

"Money makes fools outta everyone. Skies above, we got enough of 'em 'round here," the barkeep said and sent the drink down the left of the bar.

"Guess I'm a fool then, chasin' after ghosts and gold." *That's all I really know how to do, anyway...Chase leads and rumors to find my ghosts.*

The old familiar ache cut through the warmth of the drink, and he touched his necklace again. A wave of concern brushed against his mind, tugging at him to leave the saloon. Dale knocked back the last of his drink and slapped two silver scales on the counter before putting the bottles away in his pack.

"I'd best be on my way. Can't keep the Rosewater sheriff waitin'." Dale glanced at the faded embroidered name on the front of the barkeep's vest. "Thanks for the drink, Wyatt."

Dale put on his thick leather jacket before picking up his pack and the goggles resting on the stool next. He grabbed the back of Earl's shirt, and the man mumbled something in his sleep as his head lolled against his chest.

"If ya survive and collect the reward, the next drink's on me," Wyatt said and snatched the arrowhead-shaped coins and slipped them into his pocket.

Dale tipped his pale gray, wide-brimmed hat and headed for the swinging doors, dragging Earl behind him. "I'll hold ya to that."

Sand crunched underneath Dale's boots as he stepped into the heat of the day, squinting against the brightness. He headed for the line of water troughs outside the saloon.

"Time to head out, Bean. We're goin' south," Dale said and approached his mount tied to a stone post. Grunting, he lifted Earl's limp body across the back of his saddle, tying him down securely.

Dale ran his hand along the speckled gray and ocher scaly hide of the lean dragon basking in the sun. Bean's wings unfurled as he let out a throaty trill, his pink, forked tongue flicking the air. The dragon's excitement bubbled over into Dale, an imploring question flashing across his mind in scenes of the horizon and blue skies. Bean's front claws dug into the ground as Dale scratched behind one of the backward-facing horns on the dragon's head. Two metal rings from the bridle were hooked around each dark horn. Two larger green Darvus dragons tied up by the trough watched Dale and Bean with slitted amber eyes.

"Yeah, we're takin' Earl to see Bill and get us some scales before we set off after a new mark," Dale told him and untied the reins. Bean bobbed his head, tail thumping the ground. Another question rose up, showing pieces of meat. "No treats yet. Ya had some when we got here. I'll getcha somethin' nice when we get to Rosewater." Bean's disappointed whine was mirrored by the dragon's attempt to frown—lips curling back from his long teeth.

After securing Earl, Dale hauled himself onto Bean's back, adjusting a pair of thick straps in the stirrups around his boots while his legs bent against the saddle flaps just above the wings. Dale put on his worn leather gloves, and the dragon's eagerness rippled through him like a shifting breeze. Pulling a bandana over his nose, Dale slipped the goggles on. He adjusted his hat, and the magic spell along the brim activated to cling to his head. He whistled, reins held tight, and Bean lumbered down the main street of Dunesburg. People moved out of the way as the dragon raced for the takeoff area at the edge of town. Powerful muscles moved beneath the saddle, and Dale gripped Bean's sides with his legs.

Bean launched into the air, his wings beating against the blue sky. Wind rushed past as Dunesburg shrunk in the distance, and the horizon expanded in front of them like a melting band of gold. Dale kept his body against the cushioned pommel, pressure building behind his eyes. The wind spell inside his bandana flickered to life and provided him with oxygen as the air thinned. Dale's ears popped the higher they climbed, and he took deep breaths as the air became colder and thinner, his leather jacket and thick riding pants keeping him warm. Exhilaration thrummed through them both as they soared above the clouds.

Chapter 2
Smoke Trails

Seventy miles south from Dunesburg, Rosewater sat perched on the edge of the Solfaire Lake basin, with the Spineback Mountains a jagged green backdrop in the distance. Alameda's territories were a patchwork of green and brown, slashed down the middle from the Alluvialian region of the Melted Lands that extended for hundreds of miles. If Dale squinted, he could almost make out the mountain range to the west where his home was. No matter where he was in the sky, he always knew which direction it was, even though he hadn't been there in years.

Bean's concern sparked through Dale as his thoughts wandered, snapping him back to the present. "I'm good, bud," Dale said, pulling the reins to the left toward the bare landing patch behind the houses.

The dragon descended and landed with a jolt, flinging out his wings to slow himself. Dust swirled through the air as Dale urged the dragon toward the main road. Corralled terror birds in the nearby field squawked, their short, feathered wings flapping and orange beaks snapping at the air. A wagon pulled by a pair of striped, gray horses passed along the main street. The buildings cast long shadows as the sun sank, and the church bell rang out the hour.

Leaning back in the saddle, Dale removed his goggles and wiped the residue of splattered bugs off on his pants. "Let's get Earl situated."

The people of Rosewater wandered through the streets, going between the different establishments. Telegraph lines ran along like marionette strings. Several other dragon riders with brown Terracor and blue and yellow Agrosar mounts were in town. Dale glanced at the mageslinger creating ice treats outside a components shop across the way. Bean drifted toward the restaurant next to the butcher's shop that had a plume of smoke rising from the back where the meats were grilled. The smell of hickory smoke and daeodon bacon made Dale's stomach growl while Bean's yearning hunger gnawed at his insides. Dale tugged back on the reins to keep Bean from wandering into the establishment.

"No, Bean," he said, and the dragon complained with a guttural wail. "Bounty first, then food. Besides, ya know ya can't go through the door, or the whole place will come down. Can't ruin another restaurant again..." *Took a whole year to pay that one off, and we're still not welcome back in Brightwater.*

"Dale Hartwell, is that you?" a raspy voice called out from across the street.

Dale pulled Bean to a stop and spotted a plump older Alluvialian woman standing outside the haberdashery across the street. "Howdy, Meryl." He lowered his bandana and tipped his gray hat.

"Watcha doin' in these parts? I haven't seen you since I made you that hat years ago. How's it workin' for you?" Meryl's hands rested on her hips, her gray hair done up in a tight bun decorated with bright blue feathers.

"The hat's perfect. Never lost it on a flight, and the silk lining is a nice touch. I'm droppin' someone off for Bill. He in?" Dale asked.

"Far's I know, he's still at the jailhouse. Willie's there." Dale nodded and continued down the street. "Stop by when you have time, and I'll fix up that ragged coat of yours."

He threw her a tilted grin. "It ain't ragged. It's well worn."

The town jailhouse was a faded yellow stone building with a slanted tin roof and a tangled mess of violet roses growing up one side. Rumor had it that the wife of a convicted highwayman planted the bush outside the cell so her husband would have something nice to smell when they bloomed. Now, it threatened to overtake the building like a beautiful thorny, monster.

Bean stopped outside the jailhouse, and Dale unstrapped himself from the saddle and dismounted. The familiar green and brown speckled Rynlander was missing from the post out front. The leaner, brown Terracor dragon, Myst, stretched out in the shade against the building. She snorted at them, her arrowhead-shaped head resting on her crossed front feet. Bean flicked his tongue out and rumbled a greeting. Earl lifted his head, slurred muttering leaving his chapped lips. His blue eyes fluttered open, and he looked around blearily.

"Welcome back, Earl. Hope ya had some good dreams," Dale told him and untied the man from Bean's saddle.

"Wha...?" Earl muttered.

"Rivitin' stuff, Earl. Save it for yer new cellmates."

Dale dragged the man, and a heavy sack stained with red dust into the jailhouse, inhaling the scent of tobacco smoke and roses. The deputy sat at the table on the left and played with a worn deck of cards. Warm sunlight filtered in, hitting the rolltop desk and the framed black and white photographs, wanted posters, and town news pinned to the walls. Past the main room was the barred door leading to the jail cells.

Huffing, Dale dropped Earl and the bag on the floor with a *thump*. "Evenin', Willie. Bill 'round? I didn't see Creen outside."

Willie "Wilhelmina" Jack turned around in the chair, squinting at him from beneath her hat. Her round deputy badge was pinned to the front of her suspenders, and the sleeves of her blue shirt were rolled up to show off her sabercat tattoo on her brown skin. The leather shoulder holsters displayed a pair of striated dragon horn-handled revolvers. Her sharp hazel eyes shifted to him, the reed pick held between her teeth shifted to the side of her mouth.

"He went out for a bit. We've had some reports of bandits in the hills. He should be back soon," she said and laid her cards down. "What'd you bring this time?"

Dale pulled out the wanted poster and held it out to her. "Earl Carne. Bank robber. Picked him up by the Crimson Bluffs."

Earl stared up at Willie while she studied the poster. "Looks like him. Did you find where he stashed the money?"

"Caught him stashin' it." He nudged the sack with his boot. "Not sure if it's all Greentayle's stuff, but I'm sure ya can get him talkin'. He might even sing."

Willie hauled Earl to one of the empty cells, and pulled out a long key from her belt. "I'll let Bill know when he gets back. You want anything while you wait?"

A jolt of excitement from Bean hit Dale before the sounds of flapping wings did. "Looks like I didn't have to wait long. My timin' is impeccable," he said, grinning.

Dale leaned out the door to see Bean's tail wagging as he greeted the green and brown speckled dragon that landed. The rider hopped off and removed his leather helmet and goggles, brushing back his sweaty red hair. A tan formed around Bill's eyes where the goggles had been. His mount, Creen, tasted the air around Bean before she shook the dust off herself.

"Watcha doin' here, Hartwell?" the sheriff asked, his gruff voice always sounding accusatory even when he was happy.

"Bringin' ya another guest." Dale pushed off the doorframe to let Bill through. While Dale wasn't a tall man, he stood over Bill like a lanky tree.

The sheriff looked at Earl slumped in the cell. "What's the bounty?"

"One hundred and fifty gold scales," Dale told him. "An extra fifty if the stolen money is found, which I did."

"Earl Carne. That part will have to be added on by the Greentayle's law. I'll send word to their sheriff to come pick him up. Willie, get Hartwell what he's owed."

The deputy went to the iron safe by the desk, pricked her finger on one of her brass rings, and drew a small silver spell circle over the door. A hole opened as the runes parted the iron to reveal stacks of scales of different metals. She filled a pouch and handed it to Dale while the hole closed.

"Much obliged, Willie." Dale opened it and grabbed a fistful of scales, relishing the heavy clink of the coins in his palm. He closed the pouch and tucked it inside his coat.

"Ya stickin' around tonight? Need me to see if Patti has any room at the inn? It might be a few days before the Greentayle sheriff gets here."

"Nah, I'm good. I'm only stayin' the night, and I like sleepin' out in the open under the stars. It's refreshin'."

Bill dragged the sack over to his desk and sat, wiping his face with his green bandana. "Hurryin' after a new mark? There are a couple of new bounties that came in this week if ya wanna take a look. I've also been working with Sheriff Graham in Scaleburg. He's had issues with gangs smuggling some new kinds of weapons. Claims they can shoot magic."

"Guns shootin' magic? Sounds like someone's been hittin' the whiskey. Are they just mageslingers with guns?"

"The way I heard it, the guns shoot magic instead of bullets. No sign of spell circles or runes bein' used. The men have hidden the weapons, and we've not been able to find 'em or where they're gettin' 'em from. Might be good money."

"Temptin', but I've got my eye on one already. Ya know anythin' about Talon?"

Bill sat up in his chair. Willie crossed her arms, face darkening. "Are ya that desperate for money?" the sheriff asked with a furrowed brow.

"It'd set me up for a while. I'd have to catch a lot of men to make up that amount. One and done gives me more time to track down leads in Edin," Dale told him.

"I'd tell ya to stay away from this one, but yer dumb enough to go after somethin' ya shouldn't."

Dale arched an eyebrow. "Dumb? I'd call myself tenacious." Willie snorted and returned to her card game. "So, ya know anythin'?"

"Not much." Bill jerked his thumb at the wanted posters on the wall. Talon's hung in the middle, half-covered by other papers. "Reports link Talon's attacks on trains and rail ports along the major lines through the Alamedian territories near the Melted Lands. Even though Alamedian sheriffs have been after the bandit for years, they haven't been able to track him down. Sometimes soldiers have been called in to help but with no luck. The Alluvialian Councils haven't intervened although rumor has it that it's one of their people. If anythin', the attacks have dusted off the complicated tensions between us and the Alluvialians."

"Who set the bounty?"

"Heard it was Nathanial Castle."

"The Iron Baron? Why's he involved?"

"No clue. Probably some of his trains were hit. Russel would know more."

Dale put the coin bag in his pocket. "S'pose I'll go see him. Thanks for ya help."

"If ya do decide to go after Talon, be smart, Hartwell. Would hate for ya to die because ya bit off more than ya could chew," Bill said, leaning back in his chair.

"If I do, pour some good whiskey on my grave. I'll know if ya use the cheap stuff," Dale told him with a wink.

THE FIRE CRACKLED, spitting sparks toward the star-studded sky. Bean stretched out on the sandy ground dotted with soft grass, pawing at a pile of charred jackalope and large castoroides bones. The dragon crunched on a pair of small antlers. Dale leaned against Bean's side, the warm hide keeping the chill of the plains away. A sliver of moon hung among the constellations, smoky hands from the fire reaching up to try and touch the bright white light. The smell of the argan oil and aloe vera Dale had run through his short, curly hair mingled with smoke and mesquite.

Dale studied his map and compass by the firelight, balancing a tin can of chili on his knee. Several spots along the railroad lines were marked, one circled in blue indicating the most recent Talon attack twenty miles west from Rosewater. A coyote howled in the distance, and Bean stared out into the night. Dale moved his hat, and a brown dragonlizard darted out into the shadows. Blue-backed beetles skittered across the map before flying away.

"Thoughts on this, bud?" Dale asked the dragon. "Talon seems to be makin' his way down the railroads runnin' through the heart of Alamedian territories along the Alluvialian's borders. Bill said he's taken gold, guns, dragons, and magical components."

Bean lifted his head and snorted hot breath against the paper before licking up another bone with his forked tongue.

"Exactly. A bounty like that would have us sittin' pretty for a while. I could getcha some of those fancy aurochs steaks." Dale scratched Bean's underbelly, and the dragon shifted onto his side, eyes closing. "We'll head to Marrowville and see if Russel knows anythin'."

Dale dragged his pack over and fished around until he found a dented tin that once held cookies. He opened the lid with painted fields and farmers harvesting crops. Inside rattled a few blue glass marbles and his grandfather's broken pocket watch. Underneath the trinkets was a photograph with worn edges and a faded water stain. Frozen in time was his parents and his ten-year-old self. His father's smile was bright while his mother sat with the barest traces of one on her face, her metal arm catching the flashbulb light. It was a reminder of happier times before he'd watched it all crumble as his parents were dragged away.

Dale touched his necklace before putting the lid back on, remembering when his mother had given him the pendant for his eighth birthday—a time when he could hear her working in her smithy and his father had taught him about dragons and how to be a cowboy. He allowed himself a small smile. Underneath the nostalgia was the twinge of sadness that struck like an off-key note peppered with gunfire and shouting. He kept the memories and the photograph close when the hard, lonely years threatened to crush him.

They're still alive. They have to be...I'm gonna find 'em, he thought. He'd repeated the words year after year until they became worn soft to the touch. And most days he believed them, but doubt often crept in.

A rumble went through Bean as he rested his head in Dale's lap. Dale scratched the dragon behind the horns and let him lick up the remaining beans in the can. An encouraging nudge tried to buoy his spirits.

"Yer right, bud. Happy thoughts. They're alive. I'm one job closer to findin' 'em. Favor's wind might blow our way."

Dale took out a pinch of powder from a small pouch on his belt and sprinkled it into the fire, offering up a prayer to the Golden Flame as the orange tongues turned blue for a moment. Dale stared at the sky, holding the weight of his memories in his hand as firebugs darted near the flames and night creatures howled and chittered in the distance.

Chapter 3

Off the Rails

A column of smoke cut the azure sky like a scar several miles off near Marrowville. The sight made Dale uneasy as he turned Bean to the left and followed the iron vein of the tracks.

Is somethin' on fire? That's an awful lotta smoke, Dale thought. Bean let out a wavering bellow as they neared the town, and the dragon's apprehension rippled beneath his scales like a cold brook.

Clustered houses made the misshapen outline of Marrowville. The usually pristine, blue train station was obscured by blackened haze. A few dragons were grounded while people crowded the streets. Human-like shapes dotted the ground, unmoving. The wreckage of the locomotive cut into the ground, its black segmented length curled like a dead centipede with stringy metal organs spilling out. Smoke bled from the engine, and coal leaked out from the fuel car. Some of the boxcars were blasted open and oozed smoke and dark burning sludge, while others looked half-melted. A section toward the back was ripped away, steel and wooden sides torn by claw marks.

Large claw marks.

Dale brought his dragon down on the outskirts of the scene. The sulfurous smell of dragonfire and something chemical stung his eyes. Bean scratched at the dirt as Dale dismounted. His nervousness unsettled Dale. The dragon was usually calm even when they came under heavy gunfire, but now he acted as skittish as an antelope.

Somethin's got him spooked. Usually, dragons only get nervous around larger ones or alphas...The dragons that attacked must've been huge to do this.

A man stood with slumped shoulders, staring at the damage. His wide-brimmed hat was stained with age and faded from the years under the sun. A bullet hole punched_through the front of the brim.

A reddish-gray Smaugaxus dragon sat a few feet from the man, letting out a throaty shriek as she paced nervously. The frills along her long neck were on display—a sign of her unease. Dale had only ever seen Spinel anxious once when a thunderbird had flown over Marrowville five years ago.

"What happened here, Russel?" Dale asked, pushing up his goggles. *Even Spinel's on edge, and Smaugaxus aren't known for bein' afraid of much. Whatever came here must have been truly monstrous.*

Russel Debney, his gray-mustached face smudged with soot and sweat, turned toward him. The metal sheriff's shield glinted on his plaid shirt. "Watcha doin' here, Dale?" he asked, voice heavy with exhaustion. His vest, shirt, and pants seemed to swallow him whole; the years of hardship had taken away more of the man he used to be than Dale remembered.

"Dropped off a bounty with Bill yesterday and wanted to ask ya some questions, but seems ya have a lot on yer plate."

"A dragon swooped in and took out the train about an hour ago. Tore into it like it was paper. Didn't even see the beast. Halston is takin' care of gettin' the injured to Doc Mable." The sheriff sighed, pulling down the brim of his hat. Spinel stretched out her neck as she eyed Bean and snorted.

"Just one?" Dale asked with raised eyebrows. "This looks like the work of a whole posse. Or at least a few mageslingers." *What dragon is capable of doin' this? Never seen anything like this.*

"Far's I can tell. But the dragon wasn't the only thing responsible for the damage. Some of the boxcars exploded on their own, and there was some sort of corrosive bombs that melted a lot of the cargo. The survivors we pulled from the wreckage didn't see much. Just heard the roar and tearin' metal and then the explosions. And the rest...The rest are dead." Russel gestured to the bodies strewn about being dragged off by townsfolk to a horse-drawn wagon. Fear rested on his haggard features. "That dragon wasn't normal. It appeared out of nowhere. Like a ghost. Couldn't tell ya what breed."

Dale rested his hands on his waist, fingers hooked through his belt loops. He glanced back over at Bean as the dragon's anxiousness tugged at him. The dragon's tail was curled over his taloned feet, wings drawn up against his body.

"Ghost dragon's a new one. But why would a dragon be attackin' a train? Marrowville isn't in wild dragon territory."

"It wasn't just a dragon. It was Talon."

Dale's eyes snapped back to Russel. "This was *his* work? I thought he was just a train robber, not someone who'd blow up trains."

"Talon's been takin' down trains for years, and they all bear the same marks. The acid bombs are his work, destroyin' cargo he can't take. But he seems to be escalatin'. He usually targets cargo trains, not ones with civilians."

Dale approached the slashed-open boxcar, the claw marks longer than his body. He ran his gloved hand along the edge of the damage, and his fingers came away with soot. The blasted-open car still burned on the inside, and the black patches of sludge flickered with lingering flames. It wasn't a substance he recognized, and the smell burned the inside of his nose.

"What was this train transportin'?"

"Don't rightly know," Russel said, kicking at a piece of broken wood in the dirt. "This train's owned by Nathanial Castle. I was just told of its comin', not what it was carryin'. Skies above, there were civilians on the train, too. It must have been carryin' something dangerous, which makes me wonder why in the cold hells would someone have civilians on a train that's got somethin' explosive on it?" His face darkened, and he coughed, raising a kerchief to his mouth. "Never had somethin' like this happen in Marrowville. Golden Flame, help those poor souls."

Nathaniel Castle again. Is Talon targetin' his trains specifically? They must be carryin' some valuable stuff. But why blow 'em up?

Glancing down at a pile of wreckage, Dale spotted the broken body of a man next to a dead horse—or at least what looked like a man and a horse. Charred flesh was melted into the gritty ground, leaving behind the outline of what both might have looked like moments before death came. A melted gun was clutched in his hand.

Dragonfire's a terrible way to go. Dale stared at the scorch marks. *Talon has a fully sparked dragon...That complicates things. Bean's not sparked yet, and he's probably a few years from it. Not to mention the size of those claw marks. I didn't think massive dragons were real anymore. If one person and dragon could do all this, I'm gonna have to be very careful.*

Dale peered closer at the gun, stopping as he recognized part of a design near the hammer. It was a half-melted embossing of twin guns crossing a cactus flower. He knew the design better than the back of his hand. It had always hung around his mother's neck and now around his. Seeing it on something else struck him like an off-key note.

Why's that design here? And on a gun...That's Mama's symbol. He reached out to touch the metal, but it was too hot. Dale glanced at the rest of the wreckage for the symbol, but everything was too blackened and damaged to be legible.

Russel looked at the wreckage, his mouth wrinkled. "He had a bunch of guards on the train along with dragon riders, no soldiers," he said. "Most of those guards are dead or severely injured, and there aren't many survivin' passengers we can get clear statements from..."

"Were the last places hit also owned by Castle?" Dale asked.

"Bill didn't have much to go off. How can one person be movin' all that cargo on their own? Maybe Talon is just one name for different thieves hittin' different targets.

"I don't think so. I've been gettin' word from other sheriffs in the territories that have had attacks near their towns, and no one knows what to do since there are few witnesses and the stories don't make sense. Talon has always evaded all law enforcement attempts."

"It's a pattern. Now, the question is why."

Russel crossed his arms and narrowed his eyes. "*Why* are ya askin' so many questions 'bout Talon, anyway? Are ya tryin' to pick up the bounty?"

Dale avoided his gaze. "I am."

"So, that's why ya came here? For information?" The questions made Dale feel like he was thirteen again, caught trying to steal an unruly terror bird in the middle of the night to chase after his first bounty.

"Figured ya would have information on him since yer the one who keeps a keen eye on criminals. I didn't think I'd be walkin' into a scene like this."

Russel sighed, shaking his head. "Are ya doin' this for the money? If ya need some, I can lend ya some scales instead of ya takin' on somethin' so dangerous. Ya won't be any match for him."

"Perhaps, but won't know until I try. One rider and a dragon capable of destroyin' trains? Had worse odds. Remember when I helped ya several years ago with the gang who rode dire wolves and were ransackin' the nearby towns? They were almost as big as Bean. But not as smart." Bean looked over at them as he heard his name.

"Skies above, yer confidence knows no bounds. Of all the impulsive ideas ya've had, this is *the* most impulsive one."

"Impulsive seems to be workin' for me. Hasn't killed me yet. Couple close calls, but that comes with the job."

"Ya think fast on yer feet, but that's only gonna get ya so far.

Don't go riskin' yer life on somethin' so dangerous. No amount of gold is worth dyin' for. Yer parents would want ya to live, settle down, find somethin' that fulfills ya instead. Maybe use yer money to start that dragon ranch ya always talked about."

Dale met Russel's blue eyes. The older man had been the one who had promised to help him find his parents and had taken him in after they'd been taken. Russel didn't quite fill the large imprint of his flesh and blood father, but he'd been there when Dale had needed him most. When Dale started as a bounty hunter, Russel had continued to search for leads about Dale's parents even after he had left Boulder Rush for Marrowville.

"They may have wanted a lotta things, but they ain't here. They may not even be alive..." Dale muttered, the words tasting bitter before he shook his head. "I need to find out. They'd go to the ends of the world for me, so I need to do the same for 'em. And this mark is gonna be the best chance of gettin' enough money to go to Edin and follow a really promisin' lead."

"But ya could die, Dale. Don'tcha trust me to help ya find 'em? I want justice for ya folks, too. They're good people. But it's been fifteen years..."

"And I'll look for another fifteen years if I need to!" Dale snapped, hands clenching at his sides.

The faded photograph had started to take over the years of memories, the smells and sounds of home fading with each year. A dark cloud brewed as the grim realization hung on the outskirts. Bean moved to his side, his warm, scaly hide pressing against Dale's side. He gripped one of the spines along Bean's neck to keep himself from being swept away into his memories.

"Will ya help me or not, Russel?" Dale gestured to the destruction. "Best case scenario is that I bring in another dangerous criminal. Worst case...Well, just make sure someone takes good care of Bean." His dragon let out a worried whine. "It's okay, bud. I'm not goin' anywhere."

"Ya sure ya wouldn't like to have a drink and talk this

through?" Dale held Russel's gaze, jaw set. Russel let out a heavy exhale. "Stubborn. Just like yer ma." He pointed to the horizon beyond the wreckage. "Witnesses said Talon headed east toward the Melted Lands almost two hours ago. A few riders followed."

Dale stared at the flat land dotted with cacti and ocher-colored rocks. Dry grass fields and river beds ran across the canyon-pocketed landscape. Sparse trees rose up from the plains trodden by wild dragons, bison, merlstags, dire wolves, and saber-cats. Dale hadn't traversed the Melted Lands beyond its outskirts, but the rumors about the strange, warped land traveled far.

"Not much that way but the wasteland until the city of Veld." *The emptiness should make it easier to find a large dragon, assumin' the other guards didn't apprehend 'em.* "Any possibility that Talon could be hidin' out in Veld?"

"I doubt it. That's hundreds of miles away," Russel told him. "The Alluvialian Council there don't want to cause issues with us, so keepin' a notorious criminal would break the peace agreements, regardless if it's a refuge city."

"Well, if I make it back, I'll take ya up on that drink since I'm startin' a list of places to collect from," Dale said. He reached into his pack and pulled out the bottle of Malistar whiskey, holding it out to Russel. "Keep this safe for me 'til I get back. Ya look like ya could use it more than me."

Russel took the bottle, giving Dale a sad look. Dale got back onto Bean's saddle and adjusted the straps around himself. The dragon snorted as he sniffed the air and turned to the train car. Bean growled and clawed the ground, tail swishing. His wings trembled with fear, and the emotion bled through Dale, sending goosebumps along his arms.

"Please, by the heat of the Golden Flame, try not to get yerself killed or start an incident, Dale," Russel said.

"I'll do my best, but I can't make any promises," Dale said, grabbing the reins. He patted the dragon's warm flank as Bean quivered, the dragon's protests whining through Dale's mind.

"Seems we've got a scent." He put the goggles back on, squinting at the sky. *Bean's not too happy about followin' it...*

"Just...try to make it back in one piece, Dale. If not for my sake, then for yer parents'. Remember that compasses don't work the same out there, and it's easy for even experienced riders and dragons to get lost."

"Have a little faith in me. Ya were the one who taught me how to fire a gun, after all." Dale said and tipped his hat. "Thank ya for the information and everythin'. And I'm sorry about what happened here. I'm gonna try and getcha some justice."

Whistling, Dale gripped the reins, and Bean launched into the sky. The smoking wreckage below vanished as Bean rose higher, his wings beating the air. He wheeled toward the east after the scent. The rushing air cleared the smell of sulfurous dragonfire and death from Dale's nostrils.

Now, let's see if we can find this ghost.

Chapter 4

Canyon Clash

The craggy plains stretched on for miles as Bean followed the scent. Ocher-colored rocks cast short shadows under the midday sun. A large skull of a dragon lay half exposed in the sandy ground, yellowed and bleached. Antelope darted away from Bean's shadow passing over them. A herd of longhorn buffalo grazed on the patches of grassland in the distance, their large brown forms looking like spilled beans across an already sun-burned landscape.

Dale's bandana flapped against his chin, the wind blasting his ears. Bean growled as they continued east. Dale squinted at a dark shape moving in the distance on the ground in the grass fields. The faint smell of sulfuric dragonfire stung the inside of his nose, and a pained shriek cut through the air.

That looks like somethin'. Dale nudged Bean's sides, one hand going to his gun.

An injured green Darvus dragon limped across the ground on its torn and bleeding claw-tipped wings, its flank marred by dark burns. Two smaller gray Fafnyr dragons crouched across the kicked-up dirt, their riders thrown a few feet from them. Their dark green blood stained the ground. A pair of dark-winged teratornis circled overhead, their shadows falling over the injured dragons.

Dale cursed. *How can one dragon take down three? Maybe one person pretends to be Talon and draws others into an ambush. Darvus and Fafnyr's are a little bigger than Bean and bred for speed, but they're strong.*

Skies above, I hope this isn't an ambush. They're no fun when yer the one bein' ambushed.

Bean let out a worried trill as they circled above the scene. His shadow passed over the other dragons, and they shrieked at him. Dale didn't spot any of the riders moving. A wave of sadness seeped out of Bean, clenching Dale's gut. When dragons and their riders shared a bond, it was painful when it was severed suddenly. Dale had seen it before and tried not to think about what would happen to Bean if something happened to him.

"There's nothin' we can do for 'em. I'm sure Russel and the other soldiers will come lookin' for 'em," Dale muttered, urging Bean in the direction his compass pointed. *Golden Flame keep 'em warm, if they're still alive. And keep us from sufferin' their same fate.*

Canyon ridges appeared the further east they headed. The ground dropped into jagged ravines with twisted spires and sheer cliffs. Grassland turned into exposed earth as they crossed into the Melted Lands. Dale didn't see any Alluvialian riders patrolling the borders, and he wasn't prepared to run into any. While the Alluvialian lands weren't closed to Alamedians, they frowned upon people crossing their lands uninvited without taking the main roads.

This rider has no qualms about flyin' into the Melted Lands. They're either stupidly bold, or they know these lands well. Maybe that rumor about 'em bein' Alluvialian is true. What's even out here that they'd be headin' for, anyway? A place to stash the goods?

A flash of white caught Dale's eye, and he guided Bean to land behind a rocky outcrop. The landing jostled him, and Dale hopped out of the saddle, gripping the reins to pull the dragon into the shadows. Bean strained against them, bumping his head against Dale. Sharp flashes of fear hit him. Bean's amber eyes darted around, nostrils flaring as he whined.

"Sssh! Calm down, bud. Yer gonna blow our cover!" Dale hissed, clutching the dragon's head as a dark shadow passed over them. The teratornis had vanished from the skies. Dale stroked the bumpy ridge between Bean's eyes running down to his snout.

Long wings beat the air as a massive white dragon glided overhead. In its back talons was a long crate bound in netting. Large burlap sacks hung from a harness across the dragon's flank behind its wings. A rider in a dun-colored poncho sat on a saddle around the base of dragon's tree-sized neck, their face obscured by a brown scarf and a leather helmet. The dragon glided into the canyon, its tail flicking behind it like a pale snake.

Bean cowered as low to the ground as he could and trembled like a leaf. Dale's heart pounded against his ribcage, trying to flee when the rest of his body wouldn't. He'd never seen Bean so afraid, and he gripped the rocky outcrop to keep himself from being overwhelmed by the surge of draconic emotions. Dale peered around the rock, hand on his gun.

"That's one helluva dragon," he muttered and climbed back into the saddle, swallowing his own nervousness as he tightened the straps around the stirrups. *Maybe I should've just taken that drink instead...Never seen anythin' that size or color before. Ain't no breed on this continent I know that's all white. An albino? But that wouldn't have lasted long out here.*

Dale snapped the reins, but his dragon refused to move. He cursed under his breath and tried to urge Bean forward, but the dragon remained rooted to the spot.

Sighing, Dale patted Bean's neck. "C'mon, bud. We gotta go after 'em. Don't go yellow belly on me now. It's just one dragon, albeit a big one," he said and sent as many calming thoughts as he could toward his dragon.

With a reluctant whine, Bean inched forward and launched into the sky, turning toward the striated canyon after the white dragon. The ground fell away into steep cliffs and the carved paths of earth below. Russel's warning rattled around in his head, but it was hard to hear through the noise of Bean's churning emotions. Dale looked down at the compass to find the needle spinning in a circle, directionless. It was then he realized the strange energy hanging in the air, like the tension before an oncoming storm.

Never seen it do that before. He squinted up to find the sun's location, but it had moved to a different part of the sky that it hadn't been in before. *I thought we were headin' northeast, but now the sun is showin' more a southwest direction. How's that possible? The sun doesn't just magically change direction...*

Dale scanned the rocky crags, gun in hand, as Bean wheeled around a corner through the hollow, winding arteries of stone. His shadow slithered over the glittering blue-green river below. Bean slowed, head darting back and forth as he alighted on a rocky pillar jutting up from the middle of the canyon. Confusion raced around the fear until it became a tangled mess that pressed against Dale's skull. Bean clung to the rock, claws digging in as he let out a low screech, mouth snapping open and shut.

Dale gripped the reins tighter, scanning the crevices and ridges. "C'mon," Dale said. "Ya can't have lost it. Scents don't just vanish. We were right behind it."

Dale turned as a white shape melted out of the side of the canyon and slammed into Bean, its massive body blocking out the sun. Pain and panic exploded through Bean and into Dale. Screeching, Bean's claws scraped against the rocks, startling a large rock spider camouflaged against the wall. It quickly scuttled away into a crack. Bean lost his grip, and Dale was thrown out of the saddle, dangling in the air by the straps around his boots, gun clutched in his hand.

The rider, wrapped in an ocher cloak and face covered by a pale mask with dark eye slits, still sat on the back of the white dragon. Dale's heart stilled for a moment as he recognized the mask from the wanted posters. Bean lunged at the other dragon, his fearful anger roiling like hot oil through their bond. Roars filled the gorge and thundered in Dale's ears. The larger dragon rammed into Bean again, sword-like claws digging into his gray and ocher hide. The straps cut into Dale's skin as he was tossed about, scrambling to climb back into the saddle and get a clear shot at his attacker. Bean tried to dart around and bite at the other dragon, but it swatted his head away.

Dale slammed against the side of his dragon as Bean was knocked back. He hauled himself into the saddle and pulled hard on the reins to turn Bean around, adrenaline burning through him. Bean sped around the curves, the edges of his wings torn and long gashes on his side oozing green blood. Dale glanced back and didn't see Talon's white dragon pursuing them.

"C'mon, buddy!" Dale yelled as Bean's emotions spilled over. *What the Inferno kind of dragon was that?! It came out of nowhere. We gotta get someplace where it can't pin us down.*

He gripped his gun tighter, scanning the horizon. Rock formations rose up from the ground, and Bean maneuvered around them, tucking his wings in as the space grew narrower. The rocks thinned, and Dale urged the dragon upward.

Bean screeched, and Dale glanced up to see a white blur rushing toward them. It crashed into Bean and pinned him against the rocks. Howls and roars thundered through the canyon. The rider drew a gun and aimed for Dale. Bean clawed at the walls to keep from falling, but the pale dragon clamped down on his neck with large jaws and wretched him away, hurling them downward into the depths of the canyon.

Dale felt the saddle straps break and the air rush past him as he slipped off Bean's back. His stomach lurched as the sudden weightlessness wrapped around him. Thoughts jumbled together while the world blurred past, and the ground grew closer. His mother's necklace hit his cheek, glinting in the sunlight as he twisted around.

"Don't look down," his father had told Dale when he had first learned to fly. *Look straight and focus on what's in front of ya."*

The two dragons grappled against the blue sky, and Dale aimed his gun at Talon as he fell, hearing a shot before pain cracked against his skull, and the world went black.

Chapter 5
Trapped

Old dreams and new nightmares bled together in the darkness. Dale traversed them, trying to grasp at his parents before they melted from his grip in a puff of smoke. The echoes of screams and gunshots surrounded him, consuming everything he loved. A golden ouroboros slithered around the old homestead and crushed it between its coils. The guns and cactus flower emblem burned through the image. Dale tried to follow his parents as they were dragged away but found himself falling as the ground gave away with a dragon's roar.

Sunlight stung Dale's eyes as he cracked them open. Daylight came in through a window, shadows from the bars across it stretching across him. Amber glass spheres hung from the ceiling with dull sunstones gleaming inside. Hot pain gripped his skull. Dale moaned and tried to sit up but found his wrists and ankles bound with thick rope, and every part of his body felt broken.

Where am I? Am I alive? Or am I dead, and this is some sort of hell? he thought, closing his eyes. *Hell's warmer than I thought it'd be.*

Dale's thoughts lay in a scattered mess, and he tried to piece them back together. His gear and weapons were gone. He lay on a thick pallet with a woven blanket thrown over him. His torn shirt exposed large, black bruises along his stomach that hurt each time he breathed. White bandages were wrapped around his arms, and Dale wrinkled his nose at the smell of pungent salve seeping from them. Dale licked his dry lips and tasted a bitter grit sticking to his mouth.

I remember...I was fallin' and tried to shoot Talon...Bean was fightin' the white dragon. Then everythin' went black. Where's Bean?! Dale's eyes flew open. He searched for his dragon's familiar presence, but the light-headedness made it hard to focus. Everything clicked into place as he stared at the barred window. *Bars on the window. Not usually found in a welcomin' home. If this is a prison cell, it's one of the nicer ones I've been thrown into.*

A shadow moved in the corner, and a small, yellow dragonlizard slithered up the sandstone wall painted in depictions of dragons and humans, arching its wingless back up. The spiny frills around its neck flared out as it breathed. Green eyes watched him for a moment before it let out a loud hiss.

Dale tried to sit up, clenching his teeth as stiff limbs cried out and creaked. "Aren't ya an annoyin' cellmate? Ya in here for bein' irritatin'?" he muttered. He touched his neck and found the necklace gone. *Someone took all my stuff. Mama's necklace, and my family photo...Who found me, and why am I tied up? And where's the white dragon rider?*

The curtain flap parted, and a tall, lean person stepped in. He was dressed in riding pants and chaps, dark boots, and a dun-colored poncho, his black hair pulled back beneath a leather helmet. The dragonlizard crawled up the stranger's leg. Dale tried to focus on the white mask, an inkling of familiarity tugging at him, but his head swam, and nausea roiled in his stomach.

"What didja do with Bean?" Dale asked, throat dry as he spotted the gun holster at the stranger's side. The stranger didn't answer and stared down at him behind the dark lenses of the mask's eyes. "Answer me!"

The stranger approached Dale, pulling out a serrated knife from the sheath at his side. Dale stiffened, scooting back until his back hit the wall. He winced, sharp pain stabbing through his arm as one of the exposed gashes reopened. Dizziness hit him, and he struggled to keep his gaze focused.

"Who are ya? Where am I?" Dale rasped. "Didja see a giant white dragon and a rider?"

The stranger moved toward Dale quickly, grabbing his arm as blood ran down his brown skin. "Don't move," he said, his husky words rimmed with a smooth Alluviali accent. The voice wasn't as deep as Dale expected. The knife blade hovered near Dale's eye.

Whistling, the dragonlizard scurried up the stranger's arm towards the wound, claws needling Dale's skin as it jumped onto him. It sniffed the wound, licking the blood away before it let out a small burst of flames. Dale screamed as the smell of dragonfire and burning flesh hit him. His captor held him down as the dragonlizard pulled back, the gash becoming a sizzling, cauterized line.

"Bloody Golden Flame!" Dale shouted as he writhed on the pallet. *How'd he train a dragonlizard?*

Dale blinked away tears as the edges of his vision blurred. The white-masked face spun as it hovered over him, the glassy eye sockets reflecting his battered face. As his consciousness crumpled away, Dale thought he heard Bean's roar in the distance.

WHEN DALE WOKE AGAIN, it was night. The sunstones in glass spheres glowed above him, throwing iridescent light on the walls. Dragonlizards moved across the ceiling and clustered in the pools of warm sunstone light to catch moths that fluttered too close. Dale groaned and sat up. The stiffness had spread through his whole body, and his head still felt like it was splitting in two. A chill swept through the darkened window, and he pulled the thick blanket around him closer. He was still bound, but most of the cuts and bruises had been healed, leaving behind yellow patches. A dull pang of hunger punched him in the stomach.

Still alive…Did they have a mageslinger healer tend to my wounds? Would have preferred that to bein' cured by dragonlizard fire. Dale licked his lips, tasting aloe and beeswax coating them. He touched his beard and found it scragglier and thicker than he remembered. His well-oiled curly hair was now dusty and dry. *How long have I been out? My beard feels several days old.*

He spotted the earthen pitcher next to him and held it up to his nose, smelling water. Dale gulped the liquid down, some spilling down his chest and dampening his torn shirt. Cool water hit his stomach like a stone. He groaned as his shoulders locked up and resisted the movement.

On a low stone stool was a plate of grilled meat, ground corn, cornbread, and pieces of squash and green vegetables sat near him. Mouth watering, Dale gritted his teeth and rolled onto his side, forcing himself onto his knees. He scooted off the pallet to the stool and dove into the food, scarfing it down without tasting much. Dale ate every bite and licked the grease off his fingers, washing everything down with the remaining water.

He glanced at the closed door behind the thick curtain. *C'mon, Bean. Where are ya?* Dale searched for the dragon's presence. He felt the inkling of Bean's mind, his hunger and confusion puncturing Dale's thoughts. Bean recognized his nudge and grew excited. *He's alive. So, where are we?*

Grunting, Dale braced himself against the wall as he stood, legs shaking. He shuffled forward, teeth ground together against the pain. The room was sparse with a wash basin in the corner, a chamber pot, and the fur-stuffed mattress he had been lying on. With the door in arm's reach, he lost his balance, crashing to the ground. The fall jostled the contents of his stomach and made it feel like his brain was bouncing around in his skull.

Dale rolled into his side as his meal threatened to come back up. "Bloody Inferno…" he groaned and crawled to the door. The rope binding his wrists dug into his skin. *This is pitiful. Dale Hartwell, reduced to a stiff, half-alive hostage crawlin' on the ground. Guess the barkeep was right about this being foolish. Guess I was too impulsive. Note to self: canyon chases aren't ideal. I'll know for next time. If there is a next time...*

There was a metallic sound, and the door opened. The curtain moved aside, and the masked stranger stood over him. His helmet was gone, but the poncho and riding pants remained. Dale could almost feel the man's disdain behind the mask's eyeholes. He caught sight of a dark bladed hatchet hanging from the left side of the stranger's belt.

"Where's my dragon?" Dale asked and hauled himself to his knees. The stranger didn't reply. *He's wearin' the mask to hide his face, so maybe there's hope I can get out of this mess alive. Maybe I can get a good punch in and try to escape. The mask is familiar...I've seen it before.* "If ya did anythin' to him, I swear—"

"He's fine," the stranger said. "I can't say the same for you unless you start answering some questions."

Dale lunged forward, swinging his bound fists from the left. The man shifted aside and grabbed Dale's left arm, fingers digging into the still-tender wounds. Dale tried to ram his elbow at his assailant's face, but he was slammed against the wall. He struggled as the stranger pinned him by the throat, and the pain from his injuries brought blackness to the edge of his vision. The dragonlizards skittered along the ceiling and hissed.

Dale blinked, the mask in front of him pulling at his memories. A white shape, dragons roaring, the crack of a gun, and the sides of the canyon whizzing past him. He noticed for the first time a scratch on the side of the mask, almost like it'd be nicked by something. By a bullet. Cold realization drained the blood from his veins and filled them with ice.

"Yer...Talon?" Dale rasped, sweat beading across his skin. *Talon is an Alluvialian? Why would an Alluvialian be attackin' trains?*

Talon unsheathed his knife. "That isn't what my people call

me," he replied and pressed the knife under Dale's chin, the sharp point drawing a bead of blood that trickled down the blade. "If you insist on talking, you'll answer questions. And if you try to fight me again, I'll slit your throat and leave you for the coyotes."

For a moment, Dale forgot how to breathe, swallowing painfully. The glassy eyes bore into him. *He's probably gonna feed me to that monster dragon.* Dale's thoughts raced, making his head hurt. *That dragon turned invisible. I didn't dream that.*

"Why are you here?" The question pressed the knife deeper into his skin.

Dale winced. "There's a hefty price on yer head. Lotta gold."

"How did you find me?"

"Ya left a bloody trail with yer last attack. Not too hard to follow. Surprised no one's gotten this close before." Dale gave a dry laugh before the knife dug deeper into his skin, cutting the sound short. Adrenaline flooded him with heat, and his heartbeat quickened. *Rein it in, Hartwell. Can't be sarcastic when there's a knife at yer throat, and ya don't have an escape plan...*

"Are you alone?" the Alluvialian asked.

"Didja see anyone else in the canyon ready to save my ass? But with the trail of bodies ya left behind, it's only a matter behind before other bounty hunters come for ya."

"You're very cocky for someone in such a sorry state."

"It's my special skill," Dale said, managing a strained smile. He sucked in a tight breath and barely heard Russel's warning over his racing pulse. He stared at the scratch on the mask. *And it looks like I managed to nick Talon's mask. If it wasn't make of dragon horn, my bullet would've hit.*

"And why keep me alive? Ya didn't keep too many of Castle's men alive."

Talon stopped, pulling back a bit. "Did he send you? Do you work for him?"

"No. I just saw the bounty. He's just the one payin'." *So, this is about Castle. A personal grudge? Maybe I can get Talon riled up and give me an openin' to get free without gettin' stabbed or shot.* The knife grew colder, and Dale's confidence shriveled up.

A loud roar tore through the air, and Talon stiffened, looking back at the door. Dale heard other voices talking outside.

Bean! Dale thought, sensing the faint distress.

He struggled against the arm still pressed against his windpipe. The rough walls of the prison scraped against his head and back. The roar grew louder, and Dale saw Talon move before pain cracked against his chin and blackness took him back.

THE SENSATION OF FALLING, and the sound of dragons roaring woke Dale. His joints cracked as he moved. Pain throbbed through his head again in time with his pulse, and a sharp stabbing ache radiated under his chin as he swallowed. The daylight stung his eyes, and he squinted.

Still here. Must mean Talon still wants somethin' from me, and probably thinks I know somethin' about Castle, he thought. *If he keep hittin' my head, there won't be much left up there to tell him anythin' interestin'.*

A tan dragonlizard sat in the window, watching him with slitted yellow eyes before it let out a loud screech. Three other dragonlizards moved in the corners of the room, adding to the noise until it hurt Dale's ears.

"Shut up!" Dale shouted, causing them to scatter. He looked around but didn't see any plates of food. Hunger pains chewed on his insides. *Guess he's plannin' to starve me to get answers. Maybe I can catch one of those damn dragonlizards to eat...*

Dale shuffled to the chamber pot with his ankles bound and relieved himself, forehead pressed against the cool wall. He spotted his boots a few feet away with a beige dragonlizard curled inside one. Dale listened to the tiny claws scraping against the smooth sandstone walls around him. He reached out for Bean, and the dragon responded with excitement, wondering where

Dale was. He tried to answer Bean, but the dragon only gave off a sense of confusion.

What's goin' on with Bean? I can sense him, so why hasn't he come for me yet? Talon could have him chained up, but he doesn't seem to be in pain or scared. Just worried, Dale thought and looked at the door. *Maybe I can escape before Talon comes back.*

Dale tried to undo the thick ropes binding his hands, but after a few minutes of gnawing, all he had to show for his effort was sore teeth and slightly bloody gums. He looked at a dragonlizard crawling down the wall. Legs tensing, Dale lunged for the dragonlizard. It hissed and clawed at his fingers, drawing blood. He cursed as a bout of fire erupted toward his face.

I don't wanna die like this. I always hoped it'd be somethin' more dignified or heroic—goin' out in a blaze of glory while savin' some poor hapless townsfolk. Not havin' my face burned off by a dragonlizard.

Dale adjusted his bloody grip on the dragonlizard and grabbed its head. Heat bubbled up in its throat, and he aimed it at the pallet. Orange spit licked the corner, and Dale released the dragonlizard. He held the rope of the growing flame, blinking as smoke hit his eyes.

If this doesn't work, I may die because I set the room on fire and couldn't escape. That might be the worst way to go...

He coughed as heat licked his wrists, the smell of burning cloth and rope making his nose hurt. With each thread that smoldered and severed, he worried that Talon would return. The rope snapped away, and he jerked his hands away from the growing flames. A wave of dizziness hit Dale as he grabbed the chamber pot and dumped the contents onto the fire. It sizzled, and a putrid smoke rose from the blackened hole.

Dale undid the bonds around his ankles and braced himself against the wall until his dizziness subsided. He dumped the unhappy dragonlizard out of his boots, put them on, and inched toward the door. Dale tested the doorknob and found it locked.

I'm not that lucky. But maybe Talon didn't find my hidden tools.

Dale stuck his fingers inside the back of his right boot, finding the loose threading along the worn leather. He picked it loose and fished out a small pouch. A set of lockpicking tools glinted in the sunlight as he opened it.

Thank the Golden Flame that somethin' is goin' right for me. He pushed aside the curtain and studied the lock. *No magic runes around the lock at least.*

Dale inserted two picks into the keyhole, feeling the metal catching on the tumblers inside. Closing his eyes, he listened for a few seconds until he heard the faint *click*. He smiled and, putting away his lockpicking tools, tested the handle. The hinges were quiet as he opened the door, the bright light stinging his eyes. Hot wind hit his face as he stepped outside. Canyons loomed in the distance, and rocky escarpments rose like broken vertebrae around the prison. The ground a few feet from the building stopped, dropping down into the gorge. Dale looked around, finding the single brick building surrounded by sheer drops and cliffs.

Not an easy chance of escapin'. Can't see any guards, but that doesn't mean there aren't any.

As Dale turned, a bronze-skinned woman appeared around the corner of the building, knife drawn as she grabbed him. Her hair was pulled up into two coiled loops on the side of her head. She wore a red and white shawl over a dark blue dress. She gripped the front of his shirt, pushing him against the wall and holding the blade to his throat. As his head hit the bricks, a strange sense of déjà vu struck Dale.

"What did you plan to do once you broke free?" the woman asked. Her irritated tone was husky and slightly raspy, but he recognized it.

His eyes widened as he stared at her. "Wait. *Yer* Talon?!" he exclaimed.

Talon's sharp brown eyes bore into him, and her mouth curled like she was permanently disappointed. She looked to be a few years older than him, no older than thirty. *"You're* too easily surprised to be a good bounty hunter."

"It's been a rough couple of days for me—or week. I've lost track of time here. If yer gonna kill me, just push me off the cliff to spice things up." A wry smile stuck to his face as he tried to mask his churning confusion. "Knife to my throat and pinned against the wall feels too repetitive."

"I'm not going to kill you. Yet," she said and pulled the knife away, the gun in her side holster glinting under the sun.

Chapter 6
The Eyries

Talon led Dale toward a long, narrow rope bridge that extended across the ravine to the plateau on the other side. The sun sat high in the sky, pouring heat down on them. Dale looked over his shoulder and made out several other solitary prison buildings on plateaus in the canyon. Talon glared at him, and he turned to face ahead. Around the rock formations on the other side, two Alluvialian guards stood with metal spears and rifles, watching Dale.

A collection of pueblo buildings were stacked together in the distance, painted white and decorated with different plants and colorful geometric designs. Hundreds of houses were carved out of the canyon sides, and rope bridges connected the different levels to the center of the village. Green fields blanketed the rim of the canyons and the ravine. A thin waterfall plunged down into the twisting river below. Telegraph and aerial lifts lines crisscrossed over the village and along the canyon walls like dark webs.

"Mind tellin' me where I am?" Dale asked, the long walk making his muscles sore. Each step sent a jolt of pain up his spine. "Or how long I've been here?" *Bean's around here somewhere. I can sense him better now, but where is he? And where's that massive dragon?*

"The Melted Lands," Talon replied tersely. "You've been here for three days."

"*This* is the Melted Lands? I didn't think there were any settlements in this wasteland."

People stared as Dale and Talon followed the stone-paved road downhill. Women with hair tied in large loops on the side of their heads carried baskets or sat weaving vibrant garments with older women with long braids. A group of men cleaned skinned antelopes and sharpened knives. A few dragons the size of Bean sat on top of the houses, their wings spread out under the sun. A dun-striped borophagus lounged in the shadow of a building that had polished dragon scale jewelry for sale, and it barked at Dale. The throaty sound made a pen of giant terror birds squawk. Children played in the streets, and older Alluvialians meandered between shops and stalls.

Every winding street seemed peaceful, not the sort of place filled with raiders and thieves. Dale had seen a handful of Alluvialian towns and cities but never one that seemed to emerge from the landscape itself. Villagers nodded to Talon as she passed, and an air of reverence followed her. A dull headache formed as Dale took everything in. His stomach clenched at the smell of meat cooking and bread baking.

The people here must know about what Talon's been doin'. Question is, what they're doin' with all the stuff stolen from the robberies?

In between the houses, Dale spotted a flat area marked with a blue circle painted on the ground. A barrel of water and two lit torches were outside the circle. Two young Alluvialians squared off from each other, drawing spell circles in the air. The mageslingers traded attacks of ice spears and jets of fire.

No surprise that they have trained mageslingers. Wish I'd paid attention to more spells or that I could remember all the different runes. Doubt my little wind and flame spells will cause much chaos.

Talon took him to the edge of the village to a wide open area surrounded by craggy rocks. Deep caves poked out like dark eyes. Scorch marks smudged the ground, and the smell of sulfuric dragonfire burned his nose. Dozens of dragons lay curled outside, their scales blending into the landscape. Blackened bones of giant long-horned buffalo and aurochs, scattered pieces of rock spiders, and smaller bones of other animals were stacked by the caves. A few Alluvialian dragonkeepers tended to them, some armed, and a handful had mageslinger bandoliers with pouches of magical elements across their chests. They swept away the remains of their meals and scrubbing scaly hides clean.

Dragon eyries. Looks like they mostly have Badland Flyers and Smaugaxus, medium-sized and quick to spark. Probably got some larger breeds like Canyon Shadows and Agrosars, too...And whatever the Inferno that monster one is—definitely not a Canyon Shadow. But where's my dragon?

Shadows of gliding dragons fell over Dale and Talon as they took the path up to the eyries. Butterflymoths and purple hummingbirds visited the towering yucca blossoms. Smaller dragons basked in the sun and gulped down bits of bone. Bean's familiar call echoed off the cliffs, and Dale looked up to see the dragon peering down at him, tail swishing. Bean let out a low trill as he approached, keeping low to the ground. Dale broke away from Talon and scratched Bean beneath his chin, pressing his forehead against the dragon's head.

"Hey, bud. I've missed ya," Dale said, relief washing over him.

Dale saw healing red claw marks on the dragon's side and wings, and anger roiled inside him. Bean snorted and clacked his teeth together and sent Dale a soothing wave to tell him it was alright. Dale glanced through Bean's spine ridges at Talon, eyes narrowing.

That fight must've scared him good. Scared me, thinkin' that other dragon was gonna kill him. We're both lucky to have survived...

Bean curled around him, showing him flashes of an old woman and several Alluvialians tending to his wounds, and a large shadow that made him afraid yet drew him in. Mostly, there were heaps of meals Bean kept going back to that overshadowed any fear he had.

"So, it was the food that kept ya here. Yer always a sucker for a good aurochs steak." *If we could fly outta here, I could find out where I was and return later. But we won't make it far without a saddle, my weapons, a compass, or water. Can't leave without Mama's necklace, but I don't know where Talon's keepin' my things. And without knowin' where her dragon is...*

Talon shoved him toward the caves. Bean let out a forlorn whine as Dale stumbled forward.

"Don't worry. I'll be back," Dale told him.

The dragonkeepers parted as he and Talon approached a cave with blue shadows flickering inside. The walls were worn smooth by scales and dragonfire with soot and clay-painted outlines depicting dragons and people. The tunnel opened into a large cavern where an old woman with a gray braid sat by a blue fire. Claws, horns, and shells hung from the walking stick lying behind her. Creases ran along her dark leathery skin, earlobes sagging under the weight of the thick silver earrings. She woman spoke to Talon in a language Dale didn't understand. His Alluviali wasn't terrible, but the dialect the two women used was older, and he only caught a few familiar words.

Gazes darted to him. The old woman nodded and gestured with a wrinkled hand for him to sit on a flat boulder covered with a black and red blanket. Sweat formed beneath the collar of his tunic as he sat, grunting as the hard surface hit his bruised tailbone. In the corners of the room were clusters of speckled eggs resting on hot coals. A young girl with thick elbow-length leather gloves tended to the nests. The fire in the middle cast an ethereal glow inside the cavern. Each clutch was made up of five eggs the size of a small melon. Dale counted about twenty eggs in the cavern, all different colors.

A hatchery. That's why it feels like an inferno. Pa would love to see this.

The old woman said something to Talon as she poured a dark liquid from an iron teapot into three cups on a low stool next to her. She passed them to Dale and Talon. The steam gave off an aromatic, herbal smell. Dale glanced at the older woman, who smiled and took a sip.

Tea? Was she expectin' us? He drank the hot liquid, taking in the grassy and slightly sweet taste. A minty aftertaste followed. *Haven't had greenthread tea in a while. The mint's a nice touch. Still, hot tea in a hot cave seems like a bad idea...*

Setting her cup on her knee, the older Alluvialian held out a plate of wafer-thin bread made of blue cornmeal sprinkled with roasted sunflower seeds. Talon spoke hurriedly, but the gray-haired woman waved her hand, the stone beads looped around her silver bracelet jangling.

"Not that the tea and this bread aren't lovely, but I'd like to know what yer gonna do to me," Dale said. The flaky cornmeal crumbled in his mouth. "This is the strangest interrogation I've ever been subjected to. I don't think I've been fed durin' one before."

"Are you working for Castle?" Talon asked, her gaze snapping to him.

He blinked, swallowing the last sweet smokey, earthy-tasting morsel. "No. Never met the man. Ya've gone through all my stuff, so ya know I have nothin' connected to Castle besides yer wanted poster."

Talon pulled something out of her pocket. The worn metal glinted against the blue light, and the familiar twin pistols over the cactus blossom held his gaze. Dale's heart skipped a beat as he stopped eating. Talon's gun and the memory of the knife under his chin kept him from trying to snatch his mother's necklace from the woman's hand. The heat continued to gather around him, and the back of his shirt became soaked with sweat.

"If you're not working for him, why do you have this symbol?" she asked, watching his face.

"Give that back. It's just a necklace that's worth nothin' to ya." *I can't lose Mama's necklace. I don't have much left of 'em.*

"It's Castle's symbol. It's on his weapons and the crates he uses to transport goods. For you to have it means you're more connected to him than you're telling us."

"That doesn't make any sense." Dale's brow furrowed, and he wiped perspiration from his upper lip. *Did Mama copy the symbol from somewhere, and Castle's usin' it? Or are they connected somehow?* The last thought struck him like a splash of cold water.

"Either you tell us the truth, or this will be your last meal."

"I told ya, I don't know anythin'! I'm the one who wants answers."

Talon didn't answer him. Dale worked through the pieces of information she'd given him, a headache brewing behind his eyes. He loosened the top buttons of his shirt, skin too hot and the shadows from the flames moving too fast across the walls. He found himself caught between a rock and too many questions.

"That symbol is somethin' my mama made. She was...is a blacksmith. I don't know why Castle is usin' it," Dale told her, his throat dry.

Talon glanced at the older woman and spoke quietly to her. Tension built up along her muscles, her posture rigid and ready to strike at something. A faint sheen of sweat coated the women's faces, the only indication that they were affected by the heat cooking Dale from the inside out.

"Why ya raidin' his trains? Is it just because he's rich, and it's easy pickin's?"

"We don't care about his money. We're taking back what he's stolen from us."

Anger entered Talon's voice, and her gaze darted to a nearby clutch of eggs while the older Alluvialian poured more tea into her cup. Several dragonlizards chased skittering insects along the cave wall.

"So, ya have a personal grudge against Castle. What's he taken from ya? There are laws against Alamedian citizens takin' from Alluvialian lands, so why isn't yer government handlin' this?" he asked, eyes locked onto the necklace as it swung near the flames.

"A bounty hunter should know that laws don't stop everyone —especially not people like Castle," Talon said.

"Whatever's goin' on between yer people and Castle is yer business. I'm just after the gold scales that come with this job." *This has become way more than I was expectin'. If I lose the bounty, it'll hurt, but I'd rather get Mama's necklace and Bean back than be dead. But if I'm stuck here, I won't be able to find out what happened to my parents. After all this time, I finally have a decent clue...*

Talon remained silent and didn't move for a moment before she put the necklace away in her pocket. Dale's heart clenched as one of the last connections to his parents disappear out of reach. The pain growing inside his head felt like jagged rocks thumping around his brain. The food in his stomach soured.

Dale shifted as far away from the fire as he could. "So, now what?" he asked, downing the last drops of tea that did little to soothe his parched throat. "Am I gonna be brought before a Council to decide my fate, or am I gonna be yer prisoner? Or ya gonna let me cook in here?"

"This isn't a Council matter. I'm allowed to decide your fate," Talon said. "If we let you go, there's no guarantee you won't bring others here to capture me or tell Castle."

"There was a trail of wreckage leadin' here. It won't be long before someone else picks up the trail and comes here askin' questions," Dale said and set down his plate and cup. His tongue stuck to his teeth, each word feeling like cotton in his mouth.

"If you insist on leaving, I can drop you off in the wasteland and let you find your own way back. Most people only last a week or so before madness takes them. If they make it out, usually their minds are too broken to remember ever being here."

A chill prickled along Dale's skin. "What about my dragon? Bean?"

Talon raised an eyebrow. "Bean?"

"That's his name." At the mention of his name, Bean's anxious thoughts pulled at Dale. "Ya take my stuff and my freedom, but I'll be damned if ya take Bean!" His voice bounced off the walls. *It's too hot in here. Can't think straight. Gonna pass out.*

Dale's blood ran too hot, and when he blinked, he found himself watching his home fading away while he grasped aimlessly for his parents. They remained out of reach, and the fear and despair of never finding them bubbled over until it became hard to breathe.

Dale stood, lightheaded, and walked toward the entrance of the cave, straining for the faint breeze trickling in. He braced himself against the wall to keep upright. The sound of a gun being cocked made Dale freeze, his hand instinctively going to his right side where his gun usually was.

"You don't get to leave unless I say so," Talon said, her husky voice growing a serrated edge.

"Gonna change yer mind and shoot me?" Dale rasped without looking back. *Although the one time I said that, I did get shot.*

Two long-necked juvenile Smaugaxus blocked the front of the cave, barbed tongues flicking at him as their neck frills rattled. Both were smaller than Bean, but their snake-like necks could strike out quicker than Dale could run. He stopped, taking a cautious step back. Bean appeared behind them and snapped at their tails, growling. The redder one whipped around and snarled at him, sparks flying from its teeth in warning.

A loud rumble vibrated through the air, and the three dragons stopped fighting. It made the hairs on Dale's neck stand on end, Bean's fear becoming his own. The barrel of a gun pressed between his shoulder blades, and he stiffened.

"Move." Talon's command was sharper than the blade she had held to his throat.

The two Smaugaxus moved aside as Dale and Talon left the cave. As the two dragons slithered away, Bean darted for Dale. A low rumble started in the back of his throat, his slitted amber eyes locked onto Talon.

"Don't try anything," Talon told him as they stopped in the middle of the eyrie.

"Or what? Yer dragons will eat me?"

"She'll decide that."

Before a snappy remark could leave Dale's mouth, Talon stepped back into the cave, leaving him and Bean in the middle of the scorch marks. A hush spread as villagers gathered around the eyries. The remaining dragons retreated to the caves, and Bean let out a strained growl, looking up. Dale turned around to watch a massive white dragon melt out of the rock face over the eyries. Its wings unfurled until the sun was blocked out, and Dale drowned in its shadow.

Bloody Inferno, it's much bigger up close! What do they even feed this thing? Mastodons? Dale's breath quickened as the dragon lumbered toward him. He only remembered fragments of their fight in the canyon, the size of her wings and claws that batted Bean around. He let out a shuddering breath as he looked at the scorch marks beneath his boots. *One bite...That's all it'd take. Or one blast of flames, and there'd be nothin' left.*

Blue eyes the size of cannonballs watched him, hot breath from the dragon's nostrils burning his face. Long teeth glistened as its jaws parted. Faded wounds ran along its scales. Bean growled and cowered behind Dale. The dragon let out a rumble that coursed through Dale like thunder. Its scales shimmered as the colors rippled under the sun. Bean's nostrils flared, and he flattened his wings against his body. Dale flinched, and Bean's warm scales pressed into his back.

The longer Dale looked at the pale beast, the more he felt a strange sensation probing at his brain—something searching and unsettling. Snorting, the larger dragon turned and climbed back to the top of the eyrie. Bean's heightened emotions subsided, his eyes darting from Dale to the dragon lounging on the rocks.

"Guess yer dragon didn't find me appealin'," Dale said and flashed Talon a smile to hide his pounding heart and frayed nerves. He wiped his sweaty palms off on his pants, surprised that his trembling legs still held him upright as his adrenaline leaked away. "Maybe because I haven't bathed in days."

"Misae's decision to spare you was her own," Talon said, mouth pressed in a hard line.

Dale's eyes darted back to the white dragon. "Ya let the ghost dragon decide people's fates?"

Talon holstered her gun, wearing a scowl as she stepped into the sunlight. "Follow me."

He didn't move. "What are ya gonna do to me now? What does 'gettin' spared by the dragon' mean?"

Talon gave him a hard stare. Her hand rested near her gun, and Dale sensed that if he tried to test his luck, he'd wind up with a bullet in his chest or become part of the blackened stain on the ground. She gripped Dale's arm and shoved him forward, sending pain up to his shoulder.

"Hey! No need to be so rough, lady. Not unless yer payin'. If this is how ya treat yer guests, I'd hate to see how ya treat yer enemies," he snapped. "What's yer name anyway? Seems odd not knowin' it after ya've held a knife to my throat."

"My name isn't important."

Villagers parted as he and Talon left the eyries. She led him to a squat white and blue pueblo near the caves lined with flowering yucca. Small, spiny dragonlizards darted up the walls, their bronze scales turning golden in the sunlight. Bean trailed behind and stopped at the edge of the eyries with a whine.

"I'll be alright, bud. Wait here," Dale told him. *At least I hope I'll be alright...*

Talon opened the door, and the pungent smell of smoke and herbs hit Dale's nose as he stepped inside. Two women in red, white, and black shawls sat on a multicolored rug and looked up. Bowls of herbs and liquids were laid out between them, and an assortment of glass vials lined a table on the right side of the room.

They spoke to Talon, hands waving through the air. She replied and shoved Dale forward, sitting him down on a squat stool. He winced, the hard wood connecting with his tailbone and jostling his bruised ribs. The younger woman, her hair done up in two buns on the side of her head, got up and approached Dale. Her round face had a few wrinkles around her brown eyes. A polished bead necklace hung around her neck, and carved metal bracelets caught the light of the sunstone ceiling lamps. Dragon scale earrings dangled from her earlobes. She whistled, and a green dragonlizard scrambled out from under the table toward the clay stove. It spat out a spark, starting a fire beneath a metal pot.

"Remove your shirt," the older healer told him in Alamedi.

Dale hesitated for a moment before undoing his sweat-soaked shirt. The room was cooler than the hatchery, but his skin still felt hot, and the dizziness remained. Dirt and sweat had crusted along his chest, and Dale realized how stiff his clothing was. He took in the semi-healed wounds along his arms and right side.

"How did I survive my fall in the canyon anyway?" Dale asked.

"Misae caught you when you were falling in the canyon and allowed your dragon to follow us here. She thought you could be useful."

"How does a dragon know if people are useful or not? What would I be useful for?" *The bruises on my torso were from...claws.*

The older woman approached him. She poked and prodded, tilting his head to inspect his bruises. He winced as the callused fingers touched a sensitive wound on his side.

"What are they doin'?"

"Healing you," Talon told him and stood by the door, arms crossed.

"Doesn't feel like it. They're as gentle as that dragonlizard was." The pain in his side flared as she continued testing his ribs.

"I'd quit complaining before they decide to undo the healing they already started."

"Could I at least get somethin' to eat and a bath? I thought ya Alluvialians were supposed to be hospitable, yet I can't even get a comb or oil for my hair, which feels like it's a mess."

"You're worried about your hair? Do you realize the situation you're in?"

"My pa always said a man should look his best in every situation. Let me fix my hair, and I'll be the best lookin' prisoner here."

The younger woman brought over a bowl of pungent green paste, and the older healer slapped the poultice across Dale's ribs, and he cried out.

"Hold still," the younger Alluvialian said, giving him a stern look.

The older healer pricked her finger and traced circular symbols through the medicine. A cool, prickling sensation seeped beneath his skin while the mageslinger symbols glowed white for a moment, and magic crackled like static around him. Bruises faded and the pain in his ribs melted away. The dizziness abated, and his thoughts cleared. Dale sighed, the fumes of the healing herbs and salves soothing his insides with each breath.

If I make it back alive, I'll have a story Russel won't believe, he thought as the healer's strong hands massaged out the rest of his soreness.

A large moth with dark brown and gray wings fluttered in through the window. Bits of purple flashed along its body. It flew toward Talon and landed on her shoulder. She bent her head close to it, her expression changing as she listened to it chirp.

"I heard Alluvialians use special moths to send messages. Never seen one before," Dale said.

Talon turned to leave, saying something to the healers before opening the door. She pulled out the white mask from beneath her poncho, affixing it to her face. The moth fluttered outside.

"Where are ya goin'?" Dale asked and stood despite the irritated remarks from the healers. He stood in the doorway. "Ya gonna go blow up another train?"

Talon stopped in the middle of the eyrie and glanced back at him. While her face was hidden behind the mask, Dale felt a withering glare through the black eyeholes. The wind kicked up as the white dragon landed on the ground, startling the smaller ones. Her blue eyes turned on him, and Dale moved back into the healing house. Talon climbed into the saddle, and shouted something in Alluviali in the direction of the caves. Her dragon launched into the sky, the snowy scales cutting the blue like a pale scar.

The downdraft of the wings cooled Dale's sweat-coated skin. Bean trotted over and nudged Dale's hand with his sun-warmed muzzle. "Looks like we're stuck here for a bit, bud," Dale muttered and stepped into the sunlight. *Didn't learn anythin' about the symbol's connection to Castle or what Talon's takin' from the trains. Maybe I can find out while she's gone. But we can't stay. I can't lose the trail to findin' my parents after comin' this far. Probably don't stand any chance of bringin' her in...*

The old woman left the hatchery and crossed the eyries. "Try not to judge her too harshly. She doesn't treat threats lightly, both real and perceived," she said with a crackling voice. It carried the same raspy huskiness as Talon—the sound of someone who spent time around dragonfire smoke. The messenger moth rested on the front of her blouse like a living brooch.

Dale glanced at her. "You speak Alamedi?" he asked.

The old woman smiled at him with a wink. "Where do you think the girl learned it from?"

Irritation warmed Dale's skin like the beginnings of a sunburn. "Then why have her translate?"

"Because I could," she said. "Language is a powerful tool. It's important to know how to use it."

"I know some Alluviali, but I don't recognize the dialect yer usin'."

"We speak an older variation here."

"What did Talon shout before she left? Is that just part of her warm personality?"

"She told me to make sure you didn't get into trouble." The

old woman glanced at Bean and pulled out a piece of meat from the leather pouch at her side. Bean sniffed it and gently took it. "You have a strong bond with your dragon."

"I got him when I turned fifteen. Scrawny yearlin' the rancher I worked for didn't want, so he sold him cheap. Bean's been with me these past ten years."

Bean looked back at the older woman, searching for another morsel. She placed a hand on his snout, and he ruffled his wings. Happy warmth unfurled from Bean's belly. A familiar rattling sound made Dale look back at the woman. She held out the dented cookie tin to him. His breath hitched as he stared at it, fearing he was dreaming. The warm metal box in his hands felt like home. The woman's brown eyes were soft.

"I don't suppose my gun's in the box," he said, hearing the marbles rolling around inside as he clutched it close. "Or that Talon will give me back my necklace."

"You won't need your weapons here. Chochmingwa Village is safe."

He frowned, shoulders slumping. "Are ya sendin' me back to the prison house? While that was probably one of the nicer rooms I've been locked in, I'd prefer one with less dragonlizards."

"Your clothes and some of your other belongings will be at one of the inns nearby. You'll stay there for the time being. They pride themselves on being mostly dragonlizard-free."

"What about my hat? Light gray with a leather hatband?" he asked.

"We didn't find that with your things when you were brought here. Only your saddle and the bags attached to it," she replied and stepped inside the healing house. The two Alluvialian healers inclined their heads to her. The younger one, who Dale now realized had the same nose as the gray-haired woman, touched her hand as she entered.

"Damn, I really liked that hat," he muttered. *Meryl will be so mad at me for losin' one of her hats.*

Bean tried to follow him into the house, but the younger Alluvialian shooed him away before shutting the door. The dragon's whimper came through the smooth wood.

"Just who are ya? Are ya on the Elder Council, or are ya one of those Dragon Mothers Alluvialian cities have?"

"I'm both. I tend to dragon matters and occasionally offer my voice to Council matters. But most people call me Hehewuti. And Muna here tells me your name is Dale."

"It is, ma'am. And what about Talon? Can ya tell me anythin' about her? She left in a hurry, so I'm assumin' she's goin' after another one of Castle's trains."

"She'll tell you when she's ready. Traditionally, names are exchanged over tea and a meal, as I hoped would happen today, but the Sky Guardian is often impatient, especially with threats to our people."

"Sky Guardian? I don't see how destroyin' trains, stealin' property, and killin' innocent people is protectin' anyone."

Hehewuti bent down and ran her finger along the ridges of the dragonlizard's back as it skittered by her yellow and white beaded moccasins. "She isn't what you think she is. Our ways may seem different, but we've been protecting this land long before the Alamedians landed on our shores. And Misae has been around much longer. Not many tribes still follow the ancient customs of choosing a Guardian, but all Alluvialians recognize when one is chosen."

"Are there other Guardians with giant dragons in other Alluvialian cities?"

"Very few ancient dragons are left since the War of Flames. Misae has stayed with our tribe for centuries."

"I know y'all have a special connection to the dragons, but I didn't know anythin' about enormous dragons existin' outside of fairy tales."

"The world is full of strange things we humans aren't always aware of," Hehewuti said with a shrug. "The Guardian is going to be gone for a bit, so you might as well make yourself useful around here in the meantime."

"What would I be doin'? Bein' food for the dragons?" Dale asked. *Even this woman is tight-lipped about what's goin' on 'round here. Like tryin' to pry open a lake oyster.*

"I don't think they want you," the older woman replied and straightened. "You're too talkative. I could use help tending to the dragons, and you seem to do well with your own. Or, if you'd prefer, you can help with the farmers or move things throughout the village."

"Ya trust me to wander around here unbound?"

"Everyone here can handle their own. You call yourself a bounty hunter, but I think you're after something else other than our Guardian and scales. Misae seemed to think so."

"I'm just a man tryin' to make a livin'. Bounty huntin' isn't a pretty or easy job," he said.

"And what's living to you?"

"Not starvin' and havin' enough to afford a decent bed is a start."

"For a man with a dragon, with wings to soar across the country, you have very limited dreams. And from what I've heard, idealistic and impulsive."

Dale's jaw tightened as faint echoes rattled around in his head. His father's blurry face, smiling over a skillet, and the hammering from his mother's forge. Glass smashing against wood, and gunshots peppering the air. Aurochs lowing, dragons screeching, and a dusty road stretching before him. Home blurring as tears fell, the shouts of his parents ringing in his ears.

"Dreams don't keep the stomach full. It's just a means to an end." *Or pay for leads and answers. And they certainly won't bring my parents back. I can dream later once I find 'em.*

"But they keep the heart alive. Fear is the killer of dreams," Hehewuti said. "You have the look of a man running after something and haven't been able to stop chasing it. You'll have to ask yourself if you run too far for too long without rest, who will bury you when you die?"

"That'll be for me and the Golden Flame to decide," Dale muttered.

"If that's what you wish. For now, let Honovi and Muna finish healing you. Then we'll get you situated at the inn. Working here is a better option than trying to wander the Wasted Lands. It's a dangerous place to those who aren't familiar with it."

Hehewuti gave him a look that toed the line between warning and welcoming. It reminded him of the look his own grandma used to give him right before he was about to get in trouble. Dale sat back down on the stool, Honovi's exacerbated expression hovering over him as she returned to her healing magic.

Guess I'll have time to think of some way of gettin' out of here and discover what they're hidin'. And what the link is between Mama's symbol and Castle's men.

Chapter 7

Blood on the Wind

Dale swallowed the last bite of cornbread on his plate, taking a break in the shade of a towering mesquite tree at the edge of the eyrie. The slight sweetness complimented the cooked, stuffed squash, buttery slices of longhorn bison meat, frybread, and cooked cockatrice and beans. He picked up a blue corn dumpling and dipped it into the remnants of the jackalope stew. Fullness spread through his stomach, and sleep whispered its sweet siren's call in the warm breeze.

Must be some raid Talon's doin'. Either she's had to go far, or maybe someone finally caught her. The Golden Flame would have a great sense of irony if someone else managed to catch her while I'm stuck here. If I want to escape, I'll have to do it soon, he thought, brushing crumbs from his short beard.

A week had passed since Talon left. Hehewuti and the other dragonkeepers were friendly toward him, but they didn't tell him much of anything beyond the fact that he was a guest in the village. "Guest" had a strange connotation to it since he felt constantly watched when he wandered about. Every day when he left the inn, he tried to talk with stall owners and traveling traders, hoping to glean something about Talon and her dragon, but no one said anything besides glowing praises for the Sky Guardian. All he managed to learn was that the village had the best squash and boasted a variety of silver goods.

Despite it all, Dale found himself drawn to the village. His curiosity caused him to wander through the streets, taking in the mageslingers working the fields and bringing life to what everyone thought was barren land. The aerial lifts and telegraph network outpaced some of the ones he'd seen in some Alamedian settlements. While the village didn't have some of the towering buildings and monuments other Alluvialian cities had, Chochmingwa advanced down into the canyon to make the most of the earthen infrastructure.

Still, the thought of home and the empty place where his Mama's necklace used to rest on his neck kept him from becoming too entranced by the village. Bean's searching curiosity bounced around Dale like a rubber ball, but the dragon seemed content in the eyrie with the other dragons.

*Even if Bean was fully sparked, that white dragon has some sort of sway over the smaller ones. And it can turn invisible. Would it be worth it to try and grab Talon, and flee? Or try to find the telegraph station here and get a message out? Russel would tell me to be smart and live to fly another day...*Dale washed everything down with a cool glass of sumac berry juice. *Of course, with the way I'm eatin', I might get too big to fly anywhere.*

The sweet and tart liquid reminded him of the summers when his mother used to make fresh clementine and nectarine juice to keep the boiling heat at bay.

"Don't drink it all, Dale," Mama had said as she looked at the orange liquid in the glass pitcher. The warm breeze played with her bouncy black curls that framed her round face. "Leave some for your pa. He's the one actually workin' hard."

"We can always make more," Dale had replied, kicking his feet over the porch railing as he downed the juice. He looked at the clementine and nectarine trees next to the house.

Beyond the trees, his pa worked with a Fafnyr yearling that still had yellow stripes along its gray hide in a round pen. He chased it around with a rockspider silk lasso, trying to get the halter on it. His tawny brown skin was slick with sweat, smiling as he whistled at the dragon.

"C'mon, Dale! Ya said ya would help me," Pa had shouted.

"Comin'!" *Dale set the glass down and raced off to the round pen, bare feet slapping the hot sandy ground.*

Dale's hand went to his neck, but he remembered Talon still had his necklace. *Can't waste any more time here.*

A green dragonlizard darted out from behind the rocks, licking up the crumbs Dale dropped. Dale finished his food and set the blue glazed plate on the ground for the dragonlizard to lick clean. Bean looked up from where he lounged, gnawing on an aurochs' leg. The dragon trilled, his jaws stained with blood and bits of the beans that Dale had shared with him. Dale sent the image of him leaving the inn and going to the eyries to Bean, and the dragon responded with excitement.

Standing, Dale splashed water on his face from the nearby rain barrel, the sun burning down on the back of his neck. He blinked sweat out of his eyes. The week's worth of escape plans he tried to come up with all ended in him meeting a painful death or never quite coming together in his head anyway.

I could try sneakin' out tonight, but I need to get a weapon, a saddle, and riding pants. Bean's scales will tear my legs up without the proper pants. I have the dragon scales tied to sticks I can use as makeshift knives. Worst case, I try, and Bean and I are taken out in the canyon again...

He remembered the skin burns and horrible blisters left by the dragon scales from riding bareback once. The old scars were constant reminders of his foolishness. Without his rein-forced riding pants, he'd be more likely to be shredded by Bean's hide and bleed out before they made it. out of the Melted Lands—something less than ideal when planning a successful escape.

Bean spotted Hehewuti emerging from the eyries' hatchery. Bean abandoned the aurochs leg and lumbered over to her. The Dragon Mother attracted all the dragons, and Dale suspected she had seen most of them as little dragonlings hatching from eggs.

Little traitor. Dale wiped his hands off on his dirt-stained pants, and Bean ignored his disapproval. *With all the choice meats they're*

*feedin' him, it's only a matter of time before he decides he'd prefer stayin'
here.*

"Was the food good?" came a quiet voice.

Dale jumped and found Muna next to him. "When didja get
there?" he asked. "Yer as quiet as a sabercat."

Muna's cheeks reddened, and she looked at her moccasins.
"Sorry, I didn't mean to startle you. I-I just wanted to see if you
enjoyed the meal."

"I did. My compliments to the chef—especially for slippin' me
extra cornbread." Muna's cheeks darkened even more. He caught
the smile on her face as she collected the dishes.

"I'll let her know," she mumbled and glanced at Bean and
Hehewuti. "I hope Grandmother hasn't been working you too
hard."

"She has me busy from sunup to sundown, cleanin' the eyries,
gatherin' mud for brickmakin', harvestin' crops, and doin' whatever she wants. It's hard work, but nothin' I ain't used to.
Although brickmakin' was new. Hania the innkeeper is a good
teacher."

The work reminded him of his time as a cowboy, following
and corralling herds of longhorn bison and aurochs from drag-
onback—sometimes on a terror bird or even a horse since they
were cheap and agile on land. While he didn't have to wrangle
aurochs in the village, he now smelled of sulfur at the end of each
day, and his throat burned with the familiar dragonfire smoke,
making his voice raspy like Hehewuti and the others that tended
the dragons.

"You're really good with the dragons. What breed is yours?"

"No idea. Bean's some sorta mutt. Probably has a little
Terracor in him with his colorin'. Makes knowin' when he'll spark
difficult." Dale glanced at Bean, who was tasting the air around
the other dragons. "Terracors usually spark around five years old,
but Bean's ten and shows no signs yet."

"His name is Bean?"

"I didn't have much money after I got him, so I fed him chili for a while since it was cheap. Called him Bean Chili since that was his favorite thing to eat."

"You know a lot about dragons," Muna said.

"My pa had a small dragon ranch back home," Dale replied. "Learned a lot from him and then from the cowboys I worked for when I was a teenager. Always thought I'd take over the family business someday…" *Maybe I still can once I find my parents.*

Honovi shouted across the eyries from the healing house, and Muna straightened. "I'd better get going before Auntie makes me strip the prickly pears."

The young woman flashed him a smile before she jogged to the healing house. *I guess if I end up bein' imprisoned here forever, I'll get extra cornbread…*

Dale headed around the back of the eyries. A few half-asleep dragons watched him leave before closing their bright green eyes. Squatty cacti and shrubs lined the sides of the caves. Years and untold amounts of dragon claws had shaped the dusty-colored rock. He made his way to the ridge on the outskirts of the village. The top of the escarpment was used as a take-off spot for dragons to catch the warm winds sweeping up from the canyon below. He wobbled as he climbed to the top, the wind threatening to blow him over. He gripped one of the warm rocks and squinted at Chochmingwa Village below. The fields of corn blanketed the ocher plateaus, specks of bright squash nestled amongst the green like scattered gems. Ponds full of fish were glittering scales against the fields.

From the high vantage point, Dale could make out the distant watchtowers on the surrounding lip of the canyon. The river forked into the rocky innards from the waterfall that cascaded down to feed it. In the west, where the gorge narrowed and the river stretched onward, there were fewer buildings and only two watchtowers were positioned on the ridges. He pulled out a folded map and a graphite stick from a hidden pocket he'd sewn into the waistband of his pants, pressing down against the rocks. He'd drawn a rough sketch of the village and surrounding landscape. Along the edges, he marked the times when the guards changed their watch. Only the rising and setting of the sun helped him orient where he was when his compass kept spinning around in circles. The map he'd brought with him didn't have a detailed layout of the Melted Lands.

I'm not sure which direction I came from, and the compass doesn't work here, so followin' the river and the canyon would be the best escape path to take. Or I can see where the telegraph lines lead. They have to go somewhere. Gettin' a solid plan together, so Russel can't call me impulsive.

Whoops and cheers rose from the eyries as a shadow blocked out the sun before wind blasted against Dale. Dust filled the air, and he gripped the rock, coughing and shutting his eyes against the grit. Cracking an eye open, he saw Talon's white dragon wheeling around the village. The dragons in the eyries scattered into the air. Bean shuddered, his prickly anxiousness turning into slick worry that oozed out like oil.

Guess she's back. Just my luck. Dale blinked sand out of his eyes and dusted off his hair. *Wonder what stuff she's "reclaimed" this time?*

The white dragon landed on the crags and clutched a large rope-wrapped crate in her one of her clawed feet. Several rectangular boxes were strapped across her back. Misae's massive tail slammed into the rocks, claws digging in to stop herself as she landed. Her wings kicked up dirt before she settled with a rumble that shook the air. Streaks of soot and red stood out against the white scales. Talon slid from the saddle, her familiar tan poncho streaked with blood as she stumbled down the steps. She clutched her side and held a cloth-wrapped object under her arm. Hehewuti and a few of the dragonkeepers rushed to her, catching her before she fell.

Blood? Did she get injured?

Dale climbed down from the rocks. Bean clambered toward him and kept glancing back to the eyries where the white beast stood over the caves with her pale wings outspread. The smell of blood agitated Bean, and made Dale's heart quicken.

What the Inferno happened to her? Was it Castle's men? They're probably gettin' smart to her attacks. More villagers gathered around the eyries, and a group of them freed the long boxes from the dragon's saddle. *Guards will be distracted, the monster dragon is grounded, and Talon injured. Now's my chance to sneak away. Damn, my stuff is still at the inn. They're just things, but…They already took Mama's gun and necklace, and I don't want to lose anythin' else.*

He chewed his lower lip, eyes darting to Bean and into the empty canyon behind him. *"Be smart. Recklessness is the folly of men,"* Russel often said, his gravelly voice niggling in the back of Dale's mind.

"Not yet, bud," Dale muttered, a heavy exhale knocking the air from his lungs. *Even if I can't escape with Talon, maybe what I find out she's been stealin' will be worth somethin'.*

Dale and Bean returned to the shadowed eyries where villagers huddled around the white dragon and Talon. A group of guards in dragon scale and leather armor carried the crates away from the eyries. They had the same two guns and cactus flower symbol burned onto the wood, making Dale stop.

Mama's symbol. Talon wasn't lyin' about Castle usin' it. Or did Mama steal it from him? His confusion spun what he thought he knew about his parents around like a dust cyclone, obscuring what he thought was the truth. *Could it be true…?*

Two dragonkeepers removed Misae's saddle, and she let out a low rumble as she shook her neck. She lowered her head to sniff one of the sacks that had been taken from the larger crate, her jaws stained red. One of the dragonkeepers opened the sack to reveal round, blue-gray objects the size of small cannon balls. Their shells were mottled and glossy like polished stones.

Dale's eyes widened. *Dragon eggs? Is she stealin' 'em from Castle? I thought he was movin' weapons.*

The dragonkeepers gathered the eggs and took them into the

hatchery. People moved away as Misae climbed into the top of the eyries, her long claws digging into the rocks. Faded scars lined Misae's underbelly. Bean stopped and pressed against the ground, head lowered. The sharp blue eyes landed on Dale, and the strange prickling sensation moved through his skull again like a swarm of bees. The ancient dragon's stare seemed to pierce through Dale, seeing into his innermost thoughts. Dale waited for the massive jaws to snap down on him, but nothing happened.

This must be how jackalopes feel before a raptor swoops down on 'em.

A few smaller dragons peered out from the eyries. Talon sat on a boulder by the largest cave while Muna and Honovi tended to her, the white magic circles glowing near their hands. Talon ripped the blood flecked mask from her face, dark hair sticking to her forehead with sweat. Muna peeled away the torn poncho. Her dark eyes met Dale's and narrowed.

Dale followed the Dragon Mother into the hatchery, feeling the reptilian stare from above tracking his movements. The blue dragonfire threw shadows along the walls of the inner cavern, and Alluvialian voices echoed off the walls. Hehewuti sat by the fire, a blue-gray egg in her lap, running a cloth across the shell.

"I've lived many years and seen many dragon eggs," the woman said, "but each one is so unique in color, holding such life. You can feel their heartbeats through the shells."

"Why's Talon takin' eggs?" Dale asked, the surrounding heat instantly drawing sweat to the surface of his skin.

She glanced up at him. "Would you like to hold it?"

"Yer not answerin' my question."

Hehewuti lifted the egg and held it out to him. "And you're not answering mine."

Sighing, Dale hesitated before taking it. Warmth seeped through the blue shell across his palms. A faint pulse thrummed into his fingertips, and the questions inside his mind quieted. Bean's interest surrounded him, drawn to the heartbeat inside the egg.

Been a long time since I held a dragon egg. Last time was when I was a cowboy ten years ago. Nervous excitement shot through him, and for a moment, he forgot about the intense heat around him. *This blue-gray color makes me think it's a Fafnyr.*

Dragonkeepers put the other eggs in the fiery nests, creating clutches of five on the blazing coals. Thirty new ones filled the nests. One dragonkeeper approached the central fire, finger tracing a quick magic circle in the air before plunging her hand into the blue tongues. She clutched a flickering ball in her gloved palm and carried it over to a nest to feed the coals.

"Is this what Castle's been takin' from y'all?" Dale handed the egg back to the Dragon Mother.

Hehewuti gently set the egg back in her lap, tracing a small whorl pattern with a weathered finger. She glanced past him. The hairs along the back of Dale's neck prickled, and he turned to find Talon standing at the entrance of the cave, her face swathed in shadows before she stepped into the light of the dragonfire. The heels of her riding boots clacked against the ground, and smudges of blood still smeared her face. Hehewuti pulled out a pouch from her belt and handed it to Talon. The younger Alluvialian withdrew a polished stone necklace and a pair of thin silver disk earrings from the pouch and put them on. Beneath the poncho, blood oozed from a slash across her side.

"He's taken more than just dragon eggs from us," she rasped. "Illegal egg poaching is common in these parts despite the laws. Most people think this land is uninhabited beyond the wild creatures, but it's still protected."

"How do ya know these eggs are from yer lands? They could be from anywhere, and there doesn't seem to be any proof that Castle's taken 'em."

The older woman gestured for him to sit on one of the rocks, and Dale sat, wiping the sweat off his face with his bandana.

"Each clutch of eggs bears the same markings as the mother who lays them. We have been keeping track of the dragons in these lands for centuries. We can tell that these eggs were taken from nests in the Melted Lands by the shell markings. Over the years, we've seen an increase in eggs disappearing and younger dragons being taken from the wild."

Dale stared at the egg, the fuzzy image of his face reflected on the glassy surface. His pa had always kept a close eye on the twelve dragons they had at the ranch, knowing each breed and making sure Dale could recognize them by markings and calls at an early age. Every time a dragon laid eggs, his pa would bring him along to watch. His pa's smooth voice rose up in the back of his mind.

"Dragons don't raise their young when they hatch, but they protect 'em fiercely to give 'em the best chance of survivin'. May not seem like love, but I think it is," his pa had said when their dun-colored Sandghast had laid a clutch at the edge of the eyries. "Even when the hatchlin's go off on their own, the parents always remember 'em as theirs."

A bead of sweat ran down Dale's temple, stinging his eye. Bean sensed the twinge of sadness, nudging it to the surface. Dale's breath caught in his throat.

Clearing his throat, Dale asked, "What do ya plan to do with all the eggs ya've…taken back?" *Doesn't surprise me that a rich man like Castle is involved in shady stuff. Takin' eggs from the wild is probably cheaper than payin' dragon breeders. We never found the dragons that escaped from the ranch, so I wonder if the people who took Mama and Pa stole 'em, too.*

Hehewuti glanced over at one of the nests, her necklace clacking as she turned. "Very few female dragons will take eggs that aren't their own, so we hatch them and make sure they survive long enough to fend for themselves before releasing them," she said while Talon continued standing next to her. "Those that might not survive in the wild, we keep here."

"And what about the other crates? They looked more like rifle crates. Were those the weapons ya mentioned?" Dale jerked his thumb in the direction of the cave's mouth. "Did he steal those from ya, too? Or are ya just helpin' yerself to whatever he owns because he wronged ya? I noticed ya made off with those in a hurry."

"I don't take them to use them. They shouldn't end up in anyone's hands."

"He's a businessman. Last time I checked, there were no laws against sellin' weapons. Takin' dragon eggs illegally is bad, but does that justify blowin' up a train full of innocent people?"

Talon rushed around the fire toward him, teeth gritted together against the pain as she grabbed the front of his shirt. Dale almost reached for the makeshift dragon scale blade strapped to his back. "That explosion wasn't caused by me," she said. "It was one of the weapons he was transporting—a cannon. One of his guards went to use it when I was making my escape, and it malfunctioned and exploded. I was only after the weapons and his other goods. The train wasn't supposed to have civilians on it."

Dale chewed on her words, remembering the wreckage and the train's busted-open cars. "Didja hit the weapon's car and that's why it exploded?" he asked, trying to pry her scarred hands away but couldn't.

"Misae didn't use her flames on the train. She only tore into the sides to slow the train without derailing it. I was already onboard and had the other weapons when I heard the screams of the passengers." She released the front of his shirt, sweat beading across her face. "I abandoned most of the cargo and tried to leave when they fired at us. Misae even tried to sever the car that had the weapons from the rest. Then the train car exploded."

"He must have been carryin' a lotta gunpowder to make it go up the way it did..." Dale muttered, stepping back and fixing the front of his shirt.

"It wasn't the gunpowder that did it. The weapons he makes and transports aren't normal. They're too dangerous."

"All weapons are dangerous. How can the ones that he has be any different?"

"They don't just fire bullets but magic. And I think your mother helped Castle make them."

Dale laughed, shaking his head. "I've heard and seen a lot of crazy stuff since I got here, but that's the craziest thing yet. My mama didn't make anythin' like that for Castle. She never knew him, and she wouldn't be workin' with him. And guns that shoot magic? That sounds like a fantasy story."

"How can you be sure? If that's not a symbol anyone else has, then she's working with him, or he saw it and stole it. And I highly doubt he would only steal a design for his products and not the items it's attached to as well." Talon held up the necklace again, and the blue reflection of the flames melted across worn metal. "What did your mother make as a blacksmith? Where is she now?"

Her question rattled around in his head, punctured by the sounds of gunfire and yelling. His fingers twitched to snatch the necklace back and fly away, with or without a saddle. "I don't know where she is. My parents were taken fifteen years ago. Mama just made weapons, houseware items, and dragon bridles, nothin' fancy. My pa was a small-time dragon rancher. They were simple folk, not people Castle would be interested in."

"Castle's not just stealing eggs and resources or making weapons. He's taking people, too. Some of our people have gone missing over the years, and we don't know where they are, but the trails lead back to Castle. Gangs have been taking people in Alamedian territories for years, and we think it's connected to him." A sad look crossed Hehewuti's face as Talon spoke.

The twin guns and the cactus flower burned behind Dale's eyelids as he blinked. *He's takin' people? How long's he been doin' this?*

"Where did you get your gun?" Talon asked, breaking his thoughts.

"It was my mama's," Dale said and crossed his arms.

"It has the same design on the cylinder that's on Castle's crates and his weapons—and it's an older design. I don't think that's a coincidence now. Knowing that your mother was a blacksmith mageslinger, I'm sure she's making weapons for him or at least provided him the designs to do so. Yours looks slightly different than normal revolvers and a longer stock to help with the recoil, just like the newer guns."

"She wouldn't do that!" he shouted, making the dragonkeepers pause as they tended to the eggs. Anger writhed under his skin, and the heat of the hatchery seeped into his bones. Bean's whine echoed through the tunnel, the dragon sitting at the mouth of the cave. "If she was taken by Castle, she's not doin' it because she wants to. And why would he want a nobody blacksmith to make guns?"

"Inside the barrel of that gun, there are magic runes that form a spell circle. I believe Castle's using your mother's designs to make these weapons on a large scale."

Every time Dale had cleaned the barrel, he had noticed the etchings but didn't know what they were. The day their homestead had been attacked, his mother had shoved the gun into his hands before she made him run out the backdoor. She'd taught him to shoot and hunt, but he never thought to ask her more about what she was making in her forge.

Dale turned away, pinching the bridge of his nose. *Magic guns, like what Bill was talkin' about? Could that be real, or is this all just rumors? Why would Mama make somethin' like that? She only wanted to help people, not make somethin' that could cause more harm...Was she makin' it on her own or did Castle hire her to do it...?*

"Are you an *orendari?*" Talon asked.

"A what?" he snapped.

"It's what our people call mageslingers," Hehewuti told him before adding something quieter to Talon.

"Not really. I know how to make a little fire and water, sometimes a breeze when it gets too hot. But what does that have to do with anythin'?"

"Instead of needing the specific spell runes, using the required elements, and a drop of blood to activate the magic, the binding circle is inside the gun, and the bullets are specially made with an oil powder as the fuel," Talon went on. "The bullet casings are inscribed with different elemental runes found in spell circles to allow each round to shoot a different type of magic. All that's needed is a spark to activate the magic."

"Oil powder?" Dale repeated and looked back at her. "Black powder and a spark are used to fire bullets. That stuff's already volatile. Oil is for powerin' lamps, makin' pitch, and a few other things. It's a liquid. Ya can't put it in a gun and shoot it. I don't know much about mageslingin', but black powder and oil aren't components to fuel magic."

"But that's exactly what Castle's doing. It's like the spells woven into clothing and items, except there's no blood or elemental components needed. What you saw in Marrowville is only a small fraction of what can happen when these weapons malfunction or if they end up in the wrong hands. The canyon you see around our village wasn't created by time. There's a reason why the Melted Lands look the way they do. With these weapons, anyone has the power of an *orendari* at their fingertips."

Hehewuti stared at the flames, shadows filling the creases of her wrinkled face. Talon's fingers curled around the necklace and grasped her side. Despite the decades separating the two women, Dale felt the weight of history resting on them.

The Dragon Mother pulled out a bullet from the pouch around her neck and a reddish rock that had an opalescent sheen, the guns and cactus motif on the casing glinting in the light. The runes for a wind spell were etched around it.

"Oil is the lifeblood of the Earth Children and fuels magic without needing any casting elements or blood," Hehewuti said. "Our people knew of its existence long before anyone from

Alameda or any other nation across the seas did. When it hardens, it's less volatile, especially when mixed with liquid carbon, which makes it useless for magic. Our *orendari* elders would use it to commune with the Sky Mother. It wasn't used for warfare except under dire situations—always at a heavy cost.

"We knew its dangers and warned those who came to settle Tapuat and asked about it. We kept the oil fields secret, but we couldn't hide them all. There are natural springs that bubble out of the earth, but there are those who will search for the bigger reserves beneath the ground. Despite all our efforts, we keep failing to keep it out of Alamedian hands. The War of Flames two hundred years ago changed much of this landscape, all because of greed and hubris."

"And despite our people's efforts to bury any knowledge of oil magic and related weaponry since the war, it's appearing again. Because of *your* mother and Castle," Talon said, her face growing paler against the shadows.

"That's enough! She's not responsible for this!" Dale yelled.

"You're blinded by your love and idealization of your mother. How do you explain why a symbol she made is stamped onto his items or why you have an older model of the guns circulating now —one *she* made long before Castle started making them?"

Dale's hands clenched, nails digging into his palms. "Ya don't know anythin' about her. She'd never make somethin' dangerous that could hurt a bunch of people. Or work with someone who was doin' somethin' illegal. Ya said Castle's been takin' people, so he probably was responsible for my parents bein' taken."

"Regardless, your mother is connected in all this. Now that I know how Castle got his hands on the designs for these weapons, I need to find him and stop this before another war happens." Grimacing, Talon sat on a boulder, breathing heavily. Hehewuti rose and peeled back the bloodstained layers of clothing.

Dale took in the blood on her clothes, the smell of the burning train, and bodies rising in the sulfuric smoke. He knew what the white dragon was capable of and what Talon had done. Anger and fear mixed in a tumultuous storm, nausea burning the back of his throat and his eyes stinging. Bean's concern circled around Dale's mind to try and comfort him as everything he believed in and thought he knew cracked and threatened to shatter.

He turned and stepped out into the bright sunlight, the hot wind blowing away the smell of sulfur in his nose. *If they're connected, I might be able to find Mama and Pa if I find Castle. Talon's lookin' for him too, but I can't trust that she won't do somethin' terrible to Mama if she finds her. I gotta find Castle and my parents before she does.* Bean bumped against Dale's leg, dislodging the whisper of doubt perched in Dale's mind. *But could it be true...can it? And if it is, did I really know Mama at all?*

Chapter 8

Barrel of a Gun

An owl hooted outside Dale's window, and his eyes flew open. He shivered against the chill in the air as he turned over, moonlight bleeding through the curtain. The embers in the little clay heater next to the pallet burned low and cast a faint orange glow into the room. The night was quiet, broken by the nocturnal creatures outside the inn. Talon's words in the hatchery yesterday came rushing back and stoked the simmering anger still inside him. Bean groggily reached out to him, sensing Dale's frustration.

Sighing, Dale sat up, shaking off the heavy sleep encrusting him like ice. *Just an owl,* he thought, yawning and rubbing the grit from his sore eyes. *I dozed off while waitin' for midnight...Can't be fallin' asleep in the saddle while escapin'.*

Dale gathered the remainder of his things. He tied on his boots and slipped the makeshift dragon scale and fang knives through his belt loops. It wasn't a gun, but it was something. He slung his worn pack carrying all his returned belongings over his shoulder. The missing necklace still tugged at his thoughts, along with the gun missing from his side.

Maybe I should just catch a dragonlizards and find a bottle of whiskey. Might be a more effective weapon than my knives. He snuck out of the room. *Would it be worth it to try and find my gun? Or my necklace...*

The inn was quiet, and the low light of the hanging sunstone lamps filled the reception room. The Alluvialian innkeeper,

Hania, wasn't around as Dale slipped out into the night. Bean was curled against the adobe building, wings covering his body to keep out the cold. Dale touched his snout as he walked by, and the dragon lifted his head.

"C'mon, bud. We're gettin' out of here."

Bean shuffled behind him, breath rising from his nostrils. The village streets were lined with sunstone lamps on each corner. Moths gathered around the light. Stars were scattered across the dark sky, and the darkened outline of the eyries resembled a hunched dragon. Dale kept looking over his shoulder, expecting someone to stop him, but he made his way to the caves without being spotted.

Golden Flame must be watchin' over me if no one's spotted me and a large dragon sneakin' through the streets. Maybe he can spare a little more luck to get me outta here alive.

Dale saw no sign of the white dragon, and the rest of the dragons were huddled inside the warm eyries. Inside the main cave, the blue dragonfire continued to glow, a lone eerie eye against the dark. The dragonkeepers only worked during the day, so the tack chamber was empty.

Dale held up his hand to Bean. The dragon stopped, clicking his tongue against his teeth. "Wait 'round the side of the eyries." *They've gotta have my saddle and ridin' gear stashed somewhere.* Dale imagined the saddle and taking off into the sky, and Bean shook his tail eagerly.

Gripping the dragon fang knife, Dale slipped into the tack chamber. His boots scuffed against the gritty ground as he moved through the dim space. The glowing forms of the cave scorpions along the walls moved like grotesque fireflies. They gave off enough light for him to distinguish the shapes of the crates, the saddles and reins hanging on the wall, and shelves with riding gear. He inhaled the smell of oiled leather and smoke.

His fingers brushed the tough saddles until he found the familiar embossed saddle horn in the back corner. He traced the jackalope head design and hauled it off the crate. Beneath it, he found his riding pants, goggles, and Bean's reins. He half-hoped to find his hat but took a battered leather helmet instead. Dale paused to listen for anyone, hearing only the familiar nighttime sounds. He shook out his riding pants before putting them and the brown riding jacket on. The map in his trouser pocket crinkled as he moved.

So far so good. No scorpions or spiders hidin' in my gear. I'll follow the river and have water for a bit. I just have to hang on long enough to get to Russel and tell him what I've found. Maybe I can see where the telegraph lines end. That will be more reliable than the sun and the stars, which don't seem to be helpful guides here. Nothin' here makes much sense. Maybe I hit my head harder than I thought after the fight and this is all some sorta coma dream.

Dale found a coil of rock spider silk rope and a knife then left the tack chamber. Bean poked his head around the corner of jagged rocks. The moonlight turned his eyes red as the light reflected off his retinas. He trilled as he sniffed the saddle, following Dale behind the eyries.

"Let's getcha saddled up," Dale whispered and threw the saddle across the dragon's back. *Next stop will be Edin. That's where Castle's railroads run from. Mama and Pa could be there.*

As he went to tighten the straps around Bean's torso, a low rumble pressed against his eardrums and made the hairs along his neck rise. A primal fear wormed its way to the surface. Bean shrank back with a fearful whine, looking up at the top of the eyries. Dale drew his knife as a pair of red eyes cut through the darkness. Misae's usual white scales were dark, making her blend in with the rocks. A blue lamplight sprang to life in a circle of magic runes next to the dragon and illuminated Talon's lean face.

*Well, burn me alive...*Dale thought with a huff, knuckles tightening around his weapon. *Looks like the healers patched her up.*

"Was this your plan?" she asked. "Stealing a saddle and flying off into the night? It's a terrible plan. Did you think we would just let you leave after you stormed off and finding out your parents are connected to Castle and his weapons?"

"Maybe that was part of my plan all along, to do somethin' so terrible that ya wouldn't suspect I'd do it," Dale replied, gripping the knife tighter.

"You're right. It's not a terrible plan—it's a stupid one." The disdain in her voice prodded his anger, and he could almost see her eye roll in the shadows.

"Can't fault me for tryin'." *Now what, Hartwell? Don't got much to make a distraction with and she had the advantage. Could use a bit of luck right about now.*

Misae rose, and Talon jumped down from the rocks, the blue dragonfire lamp swaying with her. Dale tensed as she approached. Bean prodded his mind with questions while Dale imagined how fast he could try and stab Talon before the white dragon tore him to shreds or burned him to a crisp. Bean grumbled his disapproval, and Dale felt that was the closest the dragon could get to calling the plan foolish.

Talon stopped and glanced at Bean, then at the knife Dale held. "Hopefully, you aren't stupid enough to think that knife is going to do anything. Finish saddling your dragon and follow me."

"Is this a trick?" Dale asked before sheathing the knife and putting Bean's reins on.

She didn't reply as Misae crawled down into the middle of the eyrie. Talon hooked the lantern to her belt and climbed onto her dragon's back, holding the reins. Despite its size, the white dragon moved silently toward the take-off spot.

"Guess we're followin' her."

He settled into the familiar leather saddle, and Bean shivered with excitement to be back in the air. Dale fit the goggles on, affixed the helmet over his head, and pulled his bandana over his nose. Talon waited on the plateau, barely glancing at Dale before Misae launched off the edge like a streak of pale lightning hurtling into the canyon. The wind blasted Dale's face as the mighty wings beat the air. Bean strained against the reins.

I could just fly away if Bean's quick enough... The unknown didn't deter him, but something tugged at him to follow Talon.

Sighing, Dale squeezed Bean's sides, and the dragon shot off the ledge. The brief freefall made Dale's stomach flip. Bean's wings snapped out and caught the air currents. The dragon's elation spread through Dale in a burst of warmth. Misae flew low near the river, moonlight catching on her scales until they shimmered like crushed diamonds. Despite the terrifying memory of the monster almost killing them, Dale couldn't help but admire the ancient power flying below them. The narrow entrance between the canyon escarpments drew closer, the watchtowers coming into view. Misae tilted her body to glide through the gap and soared upward.

She's showin' off. Dale urged Bean higher into the sky, the air pressure pushing against his head and making his ears pop. *Where's she takin' me?*

The craggy landscape stretched on around them, the dark shapes of trees and rock formations looking half-melted beneath the moonlight. The Melted Lands were known for their inhospitable terrain, but even in the dark, he could see signs of life that the Alluvialians had drawn out from ruined rocks. He spared a glance at his swirling compass. It offered no direction.

They flew for a few minutes before a mesa rose before them like a dragon head breaking through the earth's crust. Talon guided her dragon toward it, slowing to land near a wide circle of eight tall rectangular stones. Several dragons half Bean's size looked up at their approach and darted into the trees. Misae took up half of the space in the clearing, drawing in her wings and tail to avoid hitting anything.

Bean landed several yards away and kept an eye on the larger dragon. Dale lifted his goggles and took in the stones and the round holes at their tops. The stone slab directly behind him was made of an opaque white stone, while the one across from it was a smooth jet-black color. The six others were made of a shimmering blue rock he couldn't identify.

"What's this place?" Dale asked as Talon dismounted.

Slinging a small sack over her shoulder, she set the lantern down, the dancing dragonfire giving her face an eerie appearance. "This is my village's sacred meeting place," she replied in a low voice. "It's where the Elders come to seek wisdom from the Sky Mother, celebrate special events, and where we release some of the adolescent dragons before they head into the wild. No violence or harm to another person is allowed on this site."

"Oh, I get it. Ya had to bring me here because ya couldn't restrain yerself from tryin' to kill me back at the village?" *She could be lyin' about this place bein' sacred, and it's just an excuse to get rid of me outside the village. I might not be useful to 'em anymore now that they know Mama was involved.*

Her eyes narrowed. "Every time you open your mouth, the thought becomes more tempting."

"Just part of my charm."

Dale hopped off Bean but didn't leave the dragon's side. The wind sang through the holes in the stones. Talon stepped closer and hurled the sack at him. Dale caught it as it thudded against his chest. Something metallic clanked inside. He found his gun, bullets, and knives inside. At the very bottom, his mother's necklace glinted, making his heart race. He ran his thumb along the familiar design.

The moment of relief was eclipsed by suspicion. "Ya didn't take anythin' from my bag, didja?"

Talon walked back to Misae. "Why would I want any of your stuff? It's just sentimental items, old weapons, and cheap clothes."

"Hey, my clothes aren't cheap. Cost me several silver scales. And my hat was *priceless*."

"Sounds like you paid too much," she muttered.

Dale holstered his gun and turned to put the other weapons in his saddlebag. He felt Misae's eyes on him, and Bean swished his tail as the tension grew. He slipped on the necklace, the medallion resting above his heart.

"Why are ya givin' me my weapons back?" he asked, pulling out his holstered gun. "And my necklace. Aren't ya worried about me havin' a dangerous magic-shootin' weapon?"

"I'm not so cruel that I would keep something so treasured from you forever. The gun won't shoot magic without oil powder, and you don't seem like you'd even know where to find the right bullets for it. You want to leave, so now's your chance. You can try to get out of the Melted Lands—and will most likely fail—or you can listen to what I have to say," Talon said. Behind her, the white dragon settled on her haunches, head towering over the seeing stones and the surrounding trees.

"And why should I trust anythin' a known outlaw says?"

"Because without me, you probably won't ever find your family."

Dale barely felt the cool metal of the gun's hammer as he drew it and aimed at Talon. She didn't flinch or reach for her own weapon. The white dragon sat up, her lips drawn back to expose her teeth. A rumbling snarl reverberated through the air, and Bean growled back. The ancient dragon loomed over Talon with a ball of blue light glowing in her chest, but Bean leapt in front of Dale, wings outspread as his growling became a roar.

"What do you think's going to happen now?" Talon asked, shadows sharpening her face. "Dragons don't know the meaning of sacred. Misae will melt you before you can shoot me."

"Probably true, but she hasn't done it yet, which makes me think yer holdin' her back," Dale told her. He stared at the giant maw, the hot breath from her nostrils hitting his face from several yards away.

Before he could blink, Talon's arm moved, and metal glinted under the moonlight. The gunshot cracked the still air into pieces, and a sharp pain jolted through his hand as the gun flew from his grasp. Bean lunged at Talon, but Misae's roar stopped him in his tracks. Dale stumbled back, clutching his hand as he looked for a wound but found nothing. His gun lay several feet away with a small dent on the bottom of the dragon horn stock. The bullet had ricocheted off into the ground several feet away. The thought of retrieving his gun was halted by his cowering dragon, and Talon's smoking gun barrel pointed at him.

"I thought ya said this was a sacred place and that ya couldn't kill or harm anyone here," Dale said, shaking his throbbing hand. *Can't believe she shot the stock. I could've lost fingers. Don't think even Russel is that good a shot...*

"You're still alive, and I didn't hit you, so I've broken no laws. I figured you'd do something truly stupid, and I was right," she told him. "Pick up your gun."

"Why? So, ya can put a bullet in me and say it was justified?"

"I'd have done that already if I wanted to. I didn't miss. Sky Mother knows no one could miss hitting such a big ego."

"Hurtful." Dale kept his gaze on her as he stooped to pick the gun up. Bean slunk over to him and pressed against his side. The fire in Misae's chest died down, but she continued to tower over them. "Since ya've made it clear that I won't be able to leave the Melted Lands, say yer piece."

Talon put her gun away. "You and I are searching for similar things—things that have been taken from us. We want those things returned. I'm proposing—"

"Sweet of ya, but I'm not interested," he said before he could stop himself and earned the most exasperated look from the Alluvialian he'd seen yet. *Careful, Hartwell, or she really will shoot ya.*

"—that we work together to find our missing people and where exactly that Castle's manufacturing his weapons, maybe even find the reason so many dragon eggs and weapons are being exported. He has his main munitions facility in Edin, but these oil magic guns are coming from another in the city I've not been able to find. I want Castle brought to justice and his guns kept from being distributed, and you want your parents back. Work with me to find him, and you'll get the answers as to where your parents might be."

Dale crossed his arms. "Did I hear that right? The mighty Sky Guardian is askin' for *my* help?" he scoffed. "I don't see why ya need me since I didn't know anythin' until ya put the pieces together for me. We seem to know about the same now—everythin' is leadin' back to Edin. I'm no mathematician, but I think those things are addin' up to somethin' pretty solid. If ya knew everythin's been comin' from Edin, why haven't ya gone there yerself?"

"Edin is almost a thousand miles from here, too far for me to go," Talon said. "As my village's Guardian, it's my duty to protect this land and its people, so I can't leave them and risk something happening to them. We've lost too many already. I hoped that by sabotaging his business that I could draw him out, but that hasn't worked. I've captured some of his men and interrogated them, but they don't know anything useful about Castle's whereabouts or what he really has planned for the goods he's transporting." Her irritation slackened into an expression Dale knew well from personal experience —dejection.

"Ah, so ya want me to do the dangerous stuff, so ya don't have to." Dale leaned back against Bean's side, the warm scales keeping the cold away. "What happened to the people ya caught before? Are they still imprisoned here? Or did ya also send them off to Edin lookin' for Castle and they never came back?" *There were other jail houses where I was held. Maybe there are others I don't know about.*

"You were the only prisoner we've had lately., and the only one I've asked to help me. Once they've served their purpose, I release them into the Melted Lands. Most make it back, but they never learn anything about this place and are mentally changed from their time in the wasteland that anything they tell people sounds like insanity."

A shiver ran down his spine as she looked at him. "Do you always do yer raids alone? Doin' somethin' that dangerous alone seems like a stupid risk—and apparently, I should know."

"Doesn't seem any more stupid than chasing after an ancient dragon and a dangerous outlaw by yourself."

The corner of his mouth twitched. "Fair point," he said.

"Despite your cockiness and impulsiveness, you're skilled with a gun, and your dragon is quick, so you'll be able to get yourself out of tough situations. I don't trust mercenaries, and I can't ask my own people to take this risk. While the Melted Lands are Alluvialian, other cities don't see much value in it. Our problems are often our own. Once I have more proof, maybe the other tribes will listen to us. But should I fall, Misae will choose another rider, and it'll be their duty to continue what I started."

"Seems like a heavy burden for one person to carry alone. Was it ever a duty ya wanted?" Dale asked and the stinging subsided from his hand. Talon's face remained unreadable, and she turned to her dragon. *Guess that's too personal.* "If Castle's the one who took my parents, I want him to face justice, too, but do ya know why he's makin' these magic guns?"

Talon placed her hand on Misae's leg. "Money ultimately, but I think he's planning something else. He's the one who sought out the knowledge to make these kinds of weapons and is funding illegal mining. There are people throughout the Alamedian lands who are discontent about living only in the territories my people gave to them when the war ended. If these guns get into the wrong hands, this land will once again descend into war, which Castle will no doubt profit from."

"Well, two hundred years was a good run without any more major wars, so it figures somethin' was bound to start brewin'."

Talon sighed. "Can you take anything seriously without joking?"

"Humor helps me get through life when my bag of scales is light, and the whiskey is low." Dale scratched his chin, the dark indigo sky lightening a bit. "So why is oil so powerful for magic? And why are ya so afraid of it? I believe it can be dangerous after seein' the train wreck, but how dangerous are we talkin'?"

"My ancestors wrote that oil is made by organic matter dying and being broken down. It's the earth's blood, made up of living things, water, earth, and fire—everything magic requires. That's what makes it so powerful."

"Not needin' to use elements or blood seems like it'd be beneficial for mageslingers and maybe create some useful things. Isn't that a good thing?" *Did Mama think about usin' it for other things before she started makin' weapons? Was she also workin' on a way to stabilize and make it safe? She wouldn't have created somethin' if she knew it was dangerous…right?*

"Just because something exists doesn't mean it should be used. Oil is a finite resource."

Talon left Misae's side and headed for the tall stones. The wind coming through the canyons swept her hair back. Dale wandered over to her, watching Misae out of the corner of his eye. Peering down into the deep ravines, he saw the silver river below and the shadowy shapes of rock spiders skittering in and out of crevices. In the distance, a dire wolf howled.

"When the War of Flames started, it was over land and resource rights," Talon began without taking her eyes off the horizon. "As the decades dragged on, desperate measures were taken to get the upper hand. Somehow, Alamedian soldiers figured out how to construct crude weapons to channel the oil they uncovered, and their *orendari* cut through the Alluvialian troops and their dragons faster than before. I'd like to say that my people knew better, but desperation got the better of my ancestors. Some used the most taboo of magics and ingested the raw oil, granting them unlimited magic for a short time at the cost of their lives, becoming Infyrni.

"Too much oil magic was used on both sides, and an eruption happened when it got out of control, igniting an oil field beneath the surface. Thousands died, and this canyon was formed, along with the other ravines across the Melted Lands. This melted wasteland was left behind. Most of the Alluvialian tribes that had been living here never returned. Our village is one of the few that remained and has been working for generations to restore the damage and make it livable again. The out-of-control magic left from the explosion made things strange, messing with people's perceptions and direction once they entered the land."

"So, that's why compasses don't work and why the sun and stars look different." She nodded. "They always taught us in school that it was the magic and dragonfire that destroyed the land," Dale said, mouth dry. Bean crouched beside him, head tilted as he looked over the edge of the mesa.

"Magic and dragonfire did cause most of the destruction. But the war didn't end because Alameda was more powerful. Your people were losing. My people ended it before we could destroy yours to stop the bloodshed. Once a truce was achieved, leaders on both sides decided it was best to seal away all knowledge of oil magic, the weapons, and the Infyrni so that the mistakes of the war wouldn't be repeated. The lands the Councils gave to the Alamedian people were ones we thought had no oil fields, but somehow Castle has been finding more."

"Seems like hidin' somethin' so important wasn't such a good idea," Dale said. "I see why ya did it, but now it seems like it's becomin' a problem again."

"It was a decision made for the greater good, but we're still paying for our blindness. That's why I must stop this from happening again, if I can. Today it's Castle, and tomorrow it may be another."

"Ya know," Dale said, a thought coming to him, "I've heard rumors of gangs usin' magic guns not too far from the town of Rosewater."

Talon met his gaze and worry clouded her face. "Then Castle's already sowing chaos. Selling those weapons will lead to more violence, and then soon, the Alamedian armies will request such weapons to 'defend' themselves. It'll only be a matter of time before the old resentments between our people are rekindled. So, I ask you again, will you help me stop this from happening?"

"Listen, I'm sorry about what happened to yer land, but I—"

Misae shifted behind Talon. The hairs along the back of Dale's neck rose as hot breath crackled along his skin. Bean squirmed behind him and kept Dale from stumbling over the edge of the mesa. Dale's face was reflected in the glowing irises, the thin membrane sliding over the dragon's eyes as she blinked. A probing presence washed over Dale like an invisible claw digging around in his mind. The canyon, its deep cliffs, and the cracks in the earth visible from the air poured through him. Lush grassland overlapped it before being consumed by fire and magic blasts. Armies clashed, dragons attacked dragons, and fiery beings shaped like humans tore through legions. An explosion nearly blinded him, leaving behind blackened scars and pits of ever-burning fire while the sky choked on smoke and the smell of sulfur.

"What's happenin'?!" Dale cried as he gripped his head, blinking to see the darkened canyon, but the bright blast remained seared behind his eyelids. "Talon, are ya doin' this?" He glanced at her, but she only watched with a stoic expression.

The flashes of fire in his mind died down, and memories he tried to keep buried swirled up in sandy clouds. The reptilian gaze pinned him to the spot, pulling back the layers of him bit by bit. Moments of his life flashed by in vivid detail. Dinners with his parents, trying to lasso dragons, and his mama being torn away while gunshots rang out. Dale tried to fight the memories as they came and tore apart the composure he'd built up over the last fifteen years. Tears formed, and he shook his head, but the invisible claws dug in deeper.

You have lost much, Dale Hartwell, a rumbling voice came, filling his mind. It resonated like a churning waterfall and clinking glass, a sound he couldn't fully decipher.

Dale's breath caught in his throat. "Bleedin' Golden Flame! What was that?!"

Talon didn't move to stop him as he stumbled into one of the nearest seeing stones. Bean called out to him, sensing his distress. The smaller dragon skirted aside as Misae lumbered toward Dale. Her snout and large teeth hovered inches from his face.

You have been offered answers, yet you are afraid of the truth, the voice said again. A hazy memory of his mama holding the gun with a mixture of pride and worry overtook his vision, something he had forgotten long ago.

"The dragon...talks?" he whispered. *I heard stories of talkin' dragons, but I thought they were just children's tales.*

Misae's scales rippled from white to jet black as she stared at the lightening sky. *I am no children's tale.*

The hot presence of the dragon probing his thoughts withdrew, and Dale collapsed on the ground, Bean's sides pressing against his head.

"Misae only speaks when she has something to say," Talon finally said.

Bean licked Dale's hand. The sudden heat on his skin jolted him from the onslaught of fragmented recollections. "What was she doin' to me? I felt...She did somethin' to me. I saw things. Was that...the explosion that created the Melted Lands?"

"Misae has lived for centuries and seen all our wars. She can see your thoughts, too. When you found us in the canyon, she sensed your intentions and spared you."

Dale blinked and looked up at Misae and Talon. "So, she knew everythin' this whole time—ya knew I was searchin' for my parents and that I didn't know Castle." He wiped the tears from his eyes. "Made me go through all that for what?"

"Knowing the truth is one thing. Hearing it from the person

themselves is another. Your memories didn't tell us the full truth. I wanted to see if you were the kind of man Misae thought you were based on your memories." Talon spread her arm out toward the canyon. "Here's your chance to leave, and I'll let you, with all the knowledge of my village, who I am, and Misae. I might even show you the safe way out if you swear you won't come after me again or tell anyone about Misae and our village."

"And what happens if I'd much rather have gold than these answers? After all, I still have to track down my folks, and that ain't cheap. I've got a reputation for bein' a good bounty hunter. Would be a shame to tarnish it now." *Not to mention that workin' with a known outlaw might hurt my credibility as a bounty hunter. If Russel found out...I guess my face wouldn't look too bad on a wanted poster.*

"If scales will buy your silence, I'll bring it up to the Council."

"Ya can't just take some from the stuff ya stole?"

"It's not mine to give away. The Council of Elders decides what to do with it."

He frowned. "Do ya think anyone will really believe ya now about Castle after all the raidin' ya've done and the Alamedian lives lost? I understand wantin' to protect what ya care about, but innocent people have died. Those are the same people who'll rejoice when yer caught and won't give a damn about yer sense of justice."

"I'll answer for the things I've done when the Sky Mother and Sun Father deem that it's my time."

A sliver of pink pushed the indigo sheet above the canyons in the distance as dawn made its presence known. The sky continued to lighten, and mist hung through the trees on the mesa.

My parents would want me to do the right thing, and I always thought that was findin' 'em. I don't know what Mama was involved in, but I don't believe she would do somethin' to hurt people intentionally. I have to find the truth.

Dale's fingers brushed the stock of his gun before he touched his necklace. His mama's bright smile was now surrounded by the smell of iron and gunpowder, smells that had always been familiar to him but now were too acrid. Dale tried to cling to the memories of better times while the nagging questions and fears circulated around in his skull.

"I s'pose there's no reason to turn ya in now. Nobody would believe me about a giant invisible dragon out in the middle of nowhere. And I don't feel right takin' money from the man who possibly kidnapped my parents." Dale stood and ran his fingers through his curly hair. "I'll help ya."

"You agreed to join me rather quickly," she said.

"It's what ya wanted, isn't it? I said I'd join ya, but that doesn't mean I trust ya. I don't agree with what ya've done, but I'll help ya get Castle because I do want answers, too."

"I would think you very foolish if you suddenly trusted me wholeheartedly."

"People already think I am, and frankly they might call me downright insane if they saw me agreein' to help ya. But before we agree to any deals, I want to know what ya intend to do with my mama once ya get yer man."

Talon tilted her head and stared at him, silent for a moment. "I suppose that will depend on what we can get out of Castle. Your mother's knowledge about how to make these weapons is just as dangerous as him manufacturing and selling them. That information can't be allowed to spread, otherwise, there will be others trying to make their own."

"I know she ain't helpin' him willingly. I'm sure she'd testify against him."

She gave a noncommittal grunt. "We'll see then. We need to catch the Iron Baron first."

"I take it ya already got a plan on how to find him or lure him out? I don't want to sound impatient to jump into my new life as an outlaw, but I don't want to waste any more time than I have to," Dale said. The shadows of the standing stones grew longer as the sun rose behind him.

"I'm waiting for word from one of my informants about his next shipment. Rumor has it that one of his top men will be going with the next shipment, and I want to capture him and see what he knows."

"Is that how ya know where Castle's trains and cargo will be? Spies?"

"Yes. I have contacts in other towns outside the Melted Lands and a few who work for him that pass along what they can, but when Castle does travel, he does so heavily protected and in secret, so I can't track him down in time. Even in Edin, he's heavily protected and rarely goes out in public."

"Could yer people in Edin find out if my parents are really there?" Dale asked with more hope in the question than he anticipated. *It's all leadin' to Edin. By the Golden Flame, am I finally gettin' closer?*

"I can ask. Give me a description of them when we get back to the village, and I'll send moths." Talon turned back to Misae and gathered up the reins. The ancient dragon lowered her neck for Talon to climb into the saddle.

Her words were like water, and he drank them up, restoring the little seedling of hope that had begun to wither. "Thank ya..." Dale turned the pendant over between his fingers. "It's funny that after all this I still don't know your name."

The woman sat back in the saddle and put on her flying helmet. "It's Kaliska."

"Kaliska, huh? Gonna be hard not to call ya Talon."

"Call me whatever you like. I have many names." She pulled out her white mask and placed it over her face. The white surface seemed to glow in the morning light. His eyes went to the dent where his bullet had hit.

"Tell me, am I the first person to have gotten close to catchin' ya?" Dale asked.

She looked at him. "You didn't catch me," she said.

"If ya hadn't been wearin' a dragon horn mask, I would've taken ya out in the canyon."

"If I had died then, you would have also died since Misae probably wouldn't have caught ya."

The chittering of dragonlings in the trees grew louder, and a few inched out into the open. Bean watched them and pawed at the ground, snorting. Misae's large head lowered toward Dale again, his face reflected in her eyes. Her muscles coiled as she moved to the edge of the mesa and launched off the edge into the canyon.

Bean perked up and glanced at Dale, tail swishing as his wings unfurled. "Guess we're stickin' 'round for a bit, bud. Then we'll head for Edin," Dale muttered and got onto his dragon's back. He took one last look at the opposite horizon where he imagined Edin to be before following Kaliska and Misae. *What have I gotten myself into this time?*

Chapter 9
To Plan a Heist

Bean's jaws opened as he yawned, his forked tongue curling against his fangs. Dale dragged a stiff brush across the dragon's scales to remove the last bits of dirt between the crevices and picked off ticks to feed to a cluster of blue and yellow dragonlizards waiting nearby. He stepped back, wiping sweat from his brow. Bean twisted around to look at him before rolling over on the ground. Dust rose as his tail thumped against the dirt, and he wriggled on his back.

Dale wrinkled his nose and frowned. "Well, now that's just rude," he said. "I spent all this time cleanin' ya and ya go and get yourself dirty again."

Bean snorted happily with what could only be described as a mischievous grin on his scaly lips. Sighing, Dale tossed the brush into the wooden bucket full of sudsy soapwood water. He stared at his pruney, callused hands before wiping them off on his pants. His fingers brushed the stock of the gun at his side, checking to make sure it was still there.

Surely, she should have somethin' by now. Or is she layin' low until the heat dies down? Dale thought, his restlessness shaking like a rattler's tail. *But this is the solidest lead I've gotten in a long time, so I can't afford to lose it. I have to find somethin' else to do with my time than practicin' my shot and scrubbin' Bean.* The dragon rolled onto his side and cocked his head in questioning. "I don't enjoy havin' to clean ya twice, bud."

Up on top of the eyries, Misae lounged with her wings

outstretched. Kaliska crouched over a map in the shade. She cleaned her hatchet, her usual riding gear traded for a simple tunic and pants. Her dark hair was done up in buns on the side of her head, the turquoise jewelry around her neck and wrists glittering in the dappled sunlight. If not for the massive dragon beside her, he could have mistaken her for one of the dragonkeepers.

Dale walked up the side of the eyrie's caves, dabbing his brow with his bandana. Misae cracked an eye open and huffed at him as he passed. Kaliska's brown eyes flicked up at him as she tested the edge of her weapon.

"I assume you're here because you want something," she said and looked back at her hatchet.

"Just wonderin' if ya have any news yet," Dale replied, standing on the edge of the shade. "It's gettin' a bit hard just waitin' around."

"How is it any different than what you did before? We can always find more work for you. Maybe we can send you to collect rock spider silk or hellbender slime."

"I'd rather not do any of those things. I didn't have much hope of any leads about where my parents were then. Now, I do, and every day we wait here feels like a chance I could lose it again."

She set the hatchet down on the rectangular piece of hide her knives rested on. Her gun was disassembled and waiting to be cleaned. The polished dragon horn handle bore marks from years past. Dale could tell it was an older revolver but a much sleeker design than the Alamedian ones he was familiar with.

Mama would love seein' the Alluvialian weapons.

"How old were you when they were taken?" Her question was softer than her usual bluntness.

Dale crossed his arms. "Ten. Men came to the house, and I remember 'em talkin' with my pa and then Mama bringin' me out to her forge. She gave me the gun and told me to run for the hills.

She seemed scared. I didn't wanna leave 'em but then I heard gunfire and shoutin' and the dragons and aurochs makin' noise. Men found us, and Mama tried to fight 'em, but they knocked her down. I ran and hid. Last I saw was her and Pa bein' dragged away while our barn was set on fire and the dragons breakin' free."

His voice caught in his throat, each word a painful barb. Time hadn't eased the pain or healed the wounds. The cold fear that had gripped him that day sunk deep into his bones when he had returned to the house to find it ransacked and the floor marred with streaks of blood. Home was empty and everything he cherished was gone, leaving him to freefall through his new reality alone. He swallowed the pain back down before it threatened to leak out of his eyes. Bean got up and called out from the bottom of the outcropping.

"I'm sorry," Kaliska said. "It's been fifteen years. How do you know that they're still alive?"

Dale sniffed, meeting her gaze. "I don't know, but I have to believe they are. No one else is lookin' for 'em. I need to know what happened to 'em even...even if it's not the answers I'm hopin' to find. Wouldn't ya do the same for yer parents?"

"I would." She adjusted the turquoise and silver bracelet around her right wrist. "I won't give up on finding my missing people. And if I can't complete it, the next Guardian will."

"Is that what happened to ya? Ya had to hunt Castle because the previous guardian did?"

"The previous Guardian was my mother. She died trying to stop a group of rustlers that raided a nearby town. She had only begun to hear whispers of Castle's illegal activities. When Misae chose me to be her rider, I began searching for the rustlers and found the connection to Castle."

"If this land is so hard to navigate, how are his men able to move through it and steal eggs, oil, and people?"

"There are safe paths for travelers to take through the Melted Lands, and the people still living here are used to the strange magical nature. There are dispelling runes that can be woven into goggles and other eyewear to help people see the land clearly. Compasses still won't work, but once you can see the sun's direction clearly, it's easier to navigate. But not a lot of people outside the Alluvialians here know this, so someone must have told Castle and helped him find the oil fields and nests."

"One of yer own helped him?"

"If it's an Alluvialian, it's not someone from this village." Her expression darkened. "This land has had enough damage done to it and things taken from it. As the only Guardian here, I have to protect it."

"Is the role always passed down to family members?" The boiling sun beat down on Dale, forcing him to step under Misae's wing.

"No. I don't know why Misae chose me, but it's an honor you can't reject—much to my father's dismay. He understands, but he fears losing me, just like my mother. If the Sky Mother wills it, I'll take Hehewuti's place when Misae deems it's time for another rider." She stared off into space for a moment before glancing at the white dragon with a wan smile.

I still don't know why a dragon should be allowed to make decisions like that, ancient or otherwise, he thought, studying the faded scars along the wing's membrane.

There are many things you will never understand, came the quiet yet all-encompassing voice of the dragon.

Dale winced at the sudden pressure in his head. "Is it always so uncomfortable when she speaks to ya?"

"It was at first, but not anymore."

If Bean started talkin' in my head, I can only imagine what it'd be about. His dragon perked up and sent him images of aurochs and chili. *Yeah, that's probably all ya'd talk about. Food.* "So, is it just ancient dragons that can talk and read minds, or is it a particular breed?"

"We don't know Misae's breed. Legend has it that it was the

first dragons that taught man to speak and use magic. There used to be more ancient dragons, but time and wars made their numbers dwindle. There were only a handful before the War of Flames. Now, I think Misae is the only one left. Most wild dragons now don't live more than a couple hundred years, and captive-bred ones maybe reach two hundred years."

The white dragon yawned, her ridge spines rattling. Sunlight created an opalescent sheen across her scales.

"That's sad," Dale muttered. "What about her invisibility? Sandwyrms, Canyon Shadows, and some dragonlizards have camouflage, but I've never seen one completely disappear, or hide its scent."

"Another one of her secrets."

"One I'm sure Castle would like to get his hands on if he's lookin' to breed dragons for his enterprises."

Kaliska's arm snapped forward, and the hatchet whizzed past him, striking the trunk of a mulberry tree behind him. Faded blade marks ran along it, and the *thunk* startled the birds nesting in its branches.

"He won't get his hands on her. He and his men have tried to lay traps in the past, but none have succeeded," she said.

"Is that how ya got injured on yer last raid? Stumbled into a trap?"

She stood, face darkening. "It was at a warehouse past Saphyre Town. Castle's men knew I was coming," she replied, voice quiet as she removed the hatchet from the tree.

"Couldn't yer dragon just read the minds of those who were lyin' in wait to warn ya?"

"She can't read every mind. Misae needs to be focused on one person at a time to know thoughts. That night, she was making sure no one outside the warehouse had discovered us. She couldn't have known what was inside."

"So, there's a good chance the next time we go after one of Castle's trains or a warehouse, he'll be expectin' us?" *I pray to the*

Golden Flame it's not another train full of civilians. How could he put innocents on there knowin' what could happen if those weapons malfunctioned?

Kaliska returned to the shade and put the hatchet. "I always think it's a trap."

"At least ya have confidence," Dale told her.

"And yet you seem to have lost yours," she replied as she reached for the pieces of her gun to reassemble.

Dale smirked at her. "Well, look who's developin' a sense of humor. It's not that I ain't confident about whatever raid we end up doin'. I've just never been on the wrong side of the law before. Sure, came close by doin' some questionable stuff, but never bandit behavior." Bean croaked, and an image of a man with a bloodied hand flitted through Dale's mind. "Buster drew first illegally in that duel, so it wasn't my fault he lost a few fingers. Plus, everyone keeps callin' me impulsive, so I'm tryin' to use a little more caution."

The breeze picked up, rustling the mulberry leaves. A large moth drifted past and landed on Kaliska's shoulder. Its brown and purple wings fluttered as it chirped at her. When it finished, Kaliska sat back with her eyes closed. Dale watched the woman's face for any sign of a reaction.

When her eyes opened again, she said, "In my bag, there's a map." Dale went over to the worn leather satchel across from her. "But be careful—"

As Dale reached inside the bag, sharp teeth sent hot pain shooting through his fingers. "Bloody Golden Flame!" he cursed and jerked his hand back, pulling out a dark green dragonlizard.

"—of the dragonlizard in there."

It let go of his fingers and soared through the air. The dragonlizard spread its forelegs and sailed away from the eyries on the red folds of skin. Bean's slitted eyes followed it as it landed in a tree.

"Why in the cold hells do ya have one of those in yer bag?" Dale hissed, sucking away the blood beading from the bite marks.

"He feels safe in there. And I did try to warn you. You'll live, or you can go see Honovi about it. I'm sure Muna would be happy to heal your flesh wound."

Dale glared at her and cautiously reached back into the bag until he found a rolled-up map. Thankfully, nothing else tried to bite him. Kaliska took the map from him and unrolled it on the ground, weighing down the corners with her knives. Dale scanned the topography of the Melted Lands and surrounding Alamedian territories. The railroad lines were drawn alongside other roads through the lands.

"In four days, one of Castle's trains will be going through Viper's Pass. It's not a route he often uses since it overlaps with the Melted Lands for a bit, but my sources say the train has more eggs and weapons on board. No civilians this time," Kaliska said and pointed to a rocky edge a hundred miles to the south.

"That's our next target?"

"Yes. Specifically, Carter McCree, one of Castle's trusted distributors who's been responsible for drilling in an oil field in this region and stealing dragon eggs in this part of the Melted Lands. He's close to Castle, and he might have the answers we're lookin' for. And if he refuses to talk, Misae will uncover the truth."

"A snatch and grab," Dale said. *Might not be Castle, but if he's got any info, it's better than nothin'.*

"There will be a squad of riders guarding the train and guards inside the train. We'll grab what weapons and eggs we can, destroy any guns we can't take with us, and get McCree out."

"When ya say destroy, do ya mean...?"

"I destroy the oil powder weapons with acid. In all the years I've done that, nothing has ever exploded. The aim is to make nothing blow up or have any casualties." Kaliska whispered to the moth and launched it into the air. It flew away until it became a speck. "Once my contact confirms when the train leaves Edin, we'll head out to wait at the Pass."

Kaliska bent over the map as a bright blue circle appeared in Edin on the far end of the southeastern side. It pulsed and remained stationary at the beginning on the railroad line in the city.

"Can't wait for more waitin'," Dale muttered. "Wouldn't it be faster to send a bird or even a dragon to deliver messages? Seems like moths are slow and likely to get eaten." *It could be longer than four days before that moth returns, if it returns at all.*

"Sometimes the old ways are best. The moths get to where they need to when they need to. Being poisonous keeps them from getting eaten, and they can take care of themselves," she told him. "The point on the map will move when the train does. One of my contacts should be the conductor on this train, and she'll slow down it down once it gets to the Pass. When we know more, there will be a more detailed plan."

"Is yer plan always jumpin' onto a train full of guards to steal stuff? And ya say my plans are poorly thought out."

"It's a little more complicated than that. I try to stop the train first, move the cargo quickly, and destroy what's left behind. Trains carry more, so they're more of a priority to hit, especially ones coming from Edin."

"Go big or go home, I guess." Dale looked at the map before letting his gaze drift to Bean. *We'll be takin' an awfully big risk, but if it gives me a chance to find my parents, I'll take it.* "Never thought I'd be hijackin' a train, but life's full of surprises."

Chapter 10
Runaway Train

Smoke trailed behind the locomotive chugging along the tracks like the acid vapors from a giant borer worm. Dale followed its movements through the spyglass, counting the riders on horseback and terror birds that followed behind the train. Dragons flew overhead through the overcast sky in an array of blue, yellow, and red scales. Under the shadow of Misae's camouflaged wing, he and Kaliska were hidden from sight. They'd been sitting on the ridge for an hour or so, waiting. Bean crouched behind them, his hot breath and nervous energy bearing down on Dale.

Twelve mounted guards outside the train. Probably more inside. Eight dragons, at least. Big Agrosars that Bean won't be able to fight alone, and the Emberghasts can shoot fire quicker than any breed, Dale thought, squinting at the caboose where a few guards waited with rifles.

Kaliska lowered the glass disk surrounded by magic text from her eye and pocketed it. "The train will reach the Viper's Pass in seven minutes. Chosovi, the conductor, confirmed that McCree is aboard," she said. "We need to be on the train before it enters the tunnel. There's an outcropping that juts out a few feet over the tracks, and we'll wait there to jump on as it passes beneath. Misae will take care of Castle's guards following the train.

"Once inside the tunnel, the riders won't be able to follow the train until it leaves the Pass. We'll have to quickly get inside, secure, as much cargo as we can, and find McCree. The train will only be in the tunnel for a few minutes, giving us the best chance to handle things inside without interference from outside."

The train got further away, and the dragons tightened their formation. "We grab him and the goods and hightail it out of there?" *Hopefully, the Dragon Mother's weather spell will hold, and the overcast skies will hide our shadows. Stayin' above the clouds will give us the element of surprise.*

"Again, a little more complicated than that." Kaliska sighed, her raspy voice echoing inside her mask. "McCree will be in one of the cars. He wears a yellow bandana and has a tattooed head. If you see him, capture him alive."

"Know what kind of tattoo it is?" Dale asked, and she glanced at him. Behind the black, glassy eyeholes, he could feel her irritated look.

"Why does that matter?"

"Lotta people have tattoos, so I just wanna make sure we grab the right one."

"It's an aurochs skull."

Dale frowned. "I was hopin' it was somethin' interestin' like a jackalope or a unicorn."

Muttering something in Alluviali, Kaliska rose from her crouch and patted Misae's underbelly. The dragon let out a low rumble. Misae shifted, the briefest outline of her body becoming visible as the coloration of her scales changed. Bean raised his head, nudging Dale's shoulder in questioning.

"It'll be fine, Bean boy. I'm sure findin' one tattooed man on a train full of armed guards and unstable weapons will be easy." *Just like it'll be easy makin' it out in one piece. Golden Flame, help us.*

Dale and Kaliska mounted their dragons and took to the skies. Dale kept Bean at a steady pace above Misae as they rose over the clouds. Kaliska cloaked herself in a camouflaging smoke. The other riders kept a diamond formation over the train, unaware of Dale and Kaliska. The train tracks cut through the flat landscape and led toward rocky cliffs and misshapen stone formations. A small gorge opened—the beginning of the Viper's Pass. Locals said a borer worm formed the mountain tunnel but later the Pass became home to a fierce wasteland viper before settlers killed it to build the railroad. Smaller wasteland vipers still made their homes in the narrower side tunnels of the pass, causing issues for trains on occasion.

Kaliska's raised left hand became visible through her camouflage cloud and signaled that they were descending. Dale's heart leapt as Misae dove down into the Pass, and Bean tucked his wings in to follow. They swerved through the rock towers, and the white dragon slowed to land on a wide outcropping several yards above the tracks. Talon marks dug into the rocks, disturbing the dirt beneath her clawed feet. Bean alighted on the wall, and Dale braced himself against the saddle against the jarring force.

"Have your dragon hide in one of the caverns while Misae takes care of the riders. Once we have the weapons, call him back. We'll grab as many as we can, but the eggs and McCree are the priority," Kaliska told him and dispelled the cloud. "Use the borer worm acid bombs like I showed you to destroy what you can't carry. When the time comes, place them in the gun crates, prick your finger on the outside of the orb, and say the incantation on it. You'll have twenty seconds to run before it goes off."

Bean moved to the edge of one of the caverns dotting the rocky pillar, and Dale dismounted. He took the bandolier of glass orbs from his dragon's saddlebag and slipped it across his chest. "I ain't a mageslinger, so hopefully, these don't randomly go off and melt me," he muttered. *Although there's a higher risk that I might break one before I have a chance to use it.* "Ya sure the stunsmoke won't affect me?"

"Did you take the antidote?"

"Yes."

"Then you'll be fine. Stop asking so many questions."

Dale huffed. "Well, 'scuse me for tryin' to be as prepared as I can be for my first train heist. Not like there was a practice run for this or anythin'."

Bean whined as the wind hit them, bringing with it the scents of the oncoming train and the riders. Kaliska dropped onto the ledge next to Dale.

"Use the speaking stone if you run into trouble. Chosovi said the weapons are in the third car. Whatever you do, try not to shoot your gun off or use excessive magic near the weapons, or it might set off the oil ammunition."

"This is all soundin' worse and worse by the minute," he muttered. "Good thing I brought my knives and sharp humor to a gunfight."

The train drew closer, and the yellow bellies of the Agrosars cut through the gray sky. Dale led Bean into the cavern and stroked his snout. The dragon clicked nervously, trying to follow Dale out as his forked tongue licked the air.

"Stay here 'til I call ya. I'll be fine, Bean boy. We've been in tougher situations than this." Scratching the dragon's jaw, Dale pressed his forehead against Bean's.

Dale stepped back onto the ledge. The train whistle pierced the air, its metallic form becoming clearer. Misae spread her wings out over the gorge to hide them from the dragons above. Dale's stomach tightened, and he watched Kaliska out of the corner of his eye.

Golden Flame, let this all go well. Let me make it out to see my parents again.

"Jump when I say to," Kaliska said, crouching. He barely heard her over the mechanical roar of the steam engine.

The Agrosars and Emberghasts flew past them, and the terror bird riders broke away as the train entered the Viper's Pass. They vanished behind the craggy walls of the pass to regroup on the other side where the gorge ended. The ground rumbled, and the screaming train pierced Dale's ears. Kaliska looked at him, but he couldn't understand what she said. She was a blur as she leapt onto the train, rolling and then righting to a crouch. The realization smacked him in the face a split second later, and he jumped off the ledge.

Dale's knees hit the metal roof as he rolled to soften the impact, but the jarring force made him lose his balance. Dale tumbled toward the edge of the train, and he grasped for something to hold onto. His curses were lost in the rushing wind as he slammed against the side of the train, holding onto the lip of the boxcar roof. The acid bombs rattled but didn't break. Pain shot through his arm as he tried to gain footing against the side, but his boots kept slipping. The wall of the Pass flew by inches from his back, and the yawning mouth of the tunnel neared.

He grasped the top of the boxcar with his other hand, teeth rattling. *Bloody Inferno! Can't go out smashed against a wall and a train. Maybe the acid bombs will break, and I'll get a quicker death than bein' mangled.*

Strong hands grabbed his, and Kaliska hauled him onto the roof. She gripped his shoulder, her braid snapping in the wind. They had landed on the fifth train car, and she had time to point ahead before the darkness of the tunnel consumed them. Kaliska's hand remained around his as a light sprang to life in front of her. The glowing orb hovered in the air and split into two, the second darting toward Dale. Kaliska pointed at him and raised two fingers before gesturing ahead.

Guess that means my car is two up. Now, if I can get to it without rolling off the train. Wonder if the guards inside know we're here with how much racket I'm makin'. She'll kill me if I'm the reason this goes south. I might just let Castle's men deal with me rather than face her wrath.

Kaliska moved forward in a crouch, her rock spider gloves helping her grip the trembling train roof. Dale pressed himself as close to the top of the train as he could and followed her cautiously. The glow of the magic light threw darting shadows across the ceiling passing overhead and the dozens of burrows carved into the tunnel walls. Kaliska jumped between the boxcars with ease, and Dale followed. He felt the *thump* of his boots on the roof as he made it to the next car.

Kaliska pointed to the next boxcar. Dale gave a thumbs up despite the oily unease in his stomach, wobbling as a sudden jolt shuddering through the train caught him off balance. A loud screeching echoed through the tunnel. Kaliska made a circular gesture with her hand and sliced downward to the roof hatch before hurrying ahead.

Dale fished the small plum-sized object from his side pouch, careful not to crush it in his grip as he pried the hatch open and chucked it against the floor. An angry shout rang out below, followed by the wheezing crack of the stunsmoke bomb going off. Dale peered into the dim car. Yellow smoke enveloped the six men inside. Panicked coughs turned into malformed cries as the smoke took hold and dropped them to the ground in its paralyzing grip. Making sure his bandana was firmly affixed over his nose and his prayer sent to the Golden Flame, Dale dropped down into the car.

Sunstone lamps swung from the ceiling, providing erratic light for the large, smoky container. Dale narrowly avoided landing on one of the prone guards lying on his back, hand frozen in place when he had been reaching for his sidearm. The stunsmoke made Dale's eyes and exposed skin tingle, but he pushed through the sensation. Thirteen crates were tied to the floor and branded with the gun and cactus flower emblem.

Unsheathing his hunting knife, Dale cut one of the boxes free and used the blade to leverage the lid open. Rows of revolvers, pistols, and rifles sat among hay to keep from jostling. All bore the familiar twin guns and cactus flower emblem on their stocks. A chill swept through Dale's veins, the faint feel of magic hanging around him like an electric charge.

Bean nudged his consciousness with worry. *It's okay, bud. Not yet,* Dale told him.

Shutting the lid, he cut the rest free and rolled the stiff bodies of the guards out of the middle of the car to lay out the rock spider-silk net from his pack. He flipped the bandolier around so the acid bombs were along his back before he hauled one of the crates onto the next, arms straining under the weight. The train lurched again, and he caught himself on the boxcar door handle before he fell.

Is that the train slowin' down? Did Kaliska make it to the front already? I'm not gonna be able to move all these boxes. Barely feels like I can move one...We'll see how effective these bombs are.

Sweat soaked through Dale's shirt by the time he managed to move the third crate to the middle. The stunsmoke thinned, and light broke through the hatch as the train left the tunnel. Cloudy sky and the rocky crags of the Viper's Pass passed overhead. He couldn't see any dragons through the clouds, but he heard a distant roar and felt Bean's anxiousness growing.

"Almost done," Dale muttered and went to haul another crate down. *Hopefully, he'll be able to carry this. Kaliska should be at the eggs by now, but I've no idea how long that'll take. Then we still need to find McCree...Do I need to set off these bombs in the other cars?*

Dale took out the speaking stone, running his thumb across the blue-green surface and the etched magic script. He chewed on his lower lip until it bled a little and wiped it across the stone while muttering the incantation. The words glowed, and the electric feeling of magic ran through his hands.

"Kaliska, can you hear me?" he asked. "I've got the guns, and I'm about to set the bombs. Where are ya?"

There was a moment of silence between his questions that stretched on too long for his liking before a muffled reply came through.

"I found—eggs, but some—s—wro—" Kaliska said, her voice almost lost over the chugging of the train and the ear-splitting whistle.

"What? What didja say?" Dale held the stone to his ear and

looked around. *How does a magic stone have a bad connection? Is somethin' interferin' with it?*

A flash of color through the boxcar door window caught his attention. Through the smoke, Dale spotted a man with a yellow bandana around his neck and a dark wide brim on his head. He and a group of five other men stood in the other car, talking and gesturing around. Beneath the man's dark hat, Dale caught sight of dark ink lines near his ears.

McCree!

"He's not—" Kaliska's voice came through again, but the screeching of the brakes drowned it out.

"I think I found him. He's in the car behind me. I'm gonna secure the guns and grab him."

"Dale, wait—"

He pocketed the stone and tied the net around the four stacked crates. Dale headed for the door, reaching for another stunsmoke bomb. The tracks raced below as he stepped across the metal connector between the cars. A half-formed plan came together in his head, the chance of failure being replaced by the fear of falling.

"If ya care about me, Golden Flame, let this work," Dale said between clenched teeth.

The train shuddered, and he was flung forward toward the door. Dale's shoulder slammed into the door handle, causing it to swing open suddenly. Five faces snapped toward him as he grabbed the doorframe to stop himself from falling. Dale made eye contact with the man in the yellow bandana.

Dale's body reacted before his brain did, and he hurled the stunsmoke bomb into the middle of the room. It shattered while Dale slammed the door shut before the guards and McCree reached him, their muffled shouts coming through the wood. They tried prying it open while Dale yanked back on the handle to keep it shut. McCree's angry face appeared through the yellow smoke.

Eventually, their struggling stopped, and they dropped to the floor. Dale slumped against the door, peering through the window as the bodies sprawled out. He unclenched his fingers from the handle and flexed his hands before pushing the door open. It was blocked by a body, but Dale managed to squeeze in.

He stood over the limp form of McCree, coughing as the smoke tickled his throat. "Ya've got a nice hat. I'll be takin' that," Dale said and plopped the hat on his head. He stared at the aurochs skull tattoo wrapped around McCree's tan head.

Grabbing McCree's burly arms, Dale hauled the man to the other car. The train slowed almost to a complete stop. The stun-smoke miasma had mostly cleared from the train compartment when Dale returned. He dropped McCree by the crates, sweat running down his back. The train stopped with a screech, and Dale unlocked the boxcar's sliding side doors to reveal steep and striated cliffs surrounding the tracks. The train sat in the middle of the gorge like a centipede in a bowl.

Dale took out the speaking stone again, muttering the inscription. "Hey, I've got McCree. Can I call Bean to get the guns?" he asked and pulled out a cord of rope to tie up McCree's hands.

"I told you to wait," Kaliska replied, panting. "*I* have McCree."

Dale stopped, the back of his neck prickling as his stomach dropped. "What? That can't be right—"

The click of a hammer behind Dale made him freeze. He turned his head to see McCree standing with a revolver pointed at him.

"So, you're the infamous Talon," he said with a sneer coated in a smooth drawl. "Looks like your luck has finally run out."

Chapter 11
Guns Go Bang

"What?" Dale managed to say, raising his hands. He clutched the speaking stone tighter as he tried to wrap his mind around what was happening.

"Is that all you know how to say?" McCree asked. He stood several inches taller than Dale, looking down on him with sharp hazel eyes.

"No. I'm just surprised that one, yer standin', and two, that ya think I'm Talon." *The stunsmoke should've worked. It took care of the others. Did this guy also take an antidote beforehand?* "Hate to break it to ya, but I'm not Talon."

"Forgive me if I don't believe the person stealing my guns and trying to take my train hostage."

Dale's brow scrunched. "Yer train? But yer..."

McCree grabbed his own forehead, and the bald head and aurochs skull peeled away to reveal a light brown face with dark curly hair that came to his shoulders. The electric buzz of magic surrounded the man for a moment before it fizzled out. Dale recognized the face from black and white newspaper photos.

"Yer Castle?" The question made his pulse quicken. "So, this was a trap..."

"And you're breaking the law, which gives me every right to shoot you where you stand." The cold barrel pressed against Dale's temple. Castle tugged the bandolier over Dale's head and set it on the ground. "You don't know how much you've cost me over the years. After you destroyed my last train, it was only a matter of time before you showed up to raid again. I figured you worked alone, but it sounds like you have someone else helping you. How many others are you working with? Where's that ghost dragon of yours I've heard so much about?"

"I ain't tellin' anythin' to the man who'd take precautions for himself and not for his men." Dale's eyes darted to the men twitching and lying on the floor, the effects of the stunsmoke beginning to wear off.

Castle shrugged, the pearl handle of his gun flashing as the light of the sunstones hit it. "Sacrifices are made in the name of business. I knew you couldn't get all my men, so I took the risk that only a few would be hit. You're certainly not who I expected the infamous bandit to be. You're less intimidating without your mask."

"I don't have a mask 'cause I ain't Talon," Dale told him. *Maybe I can apprehend him instead without havin' my brains blown out, if the Golden Flame's warmth will smile on me.*

Castle regarded him with a cool stare. "What was your plan for my guns? I'm assuming you also came for the eggs, too," he said.

"*Yer* the one stealin' things that ain't yers to take and creatin' weapons that ya shouldn't be makin'."

"Oh, so you're a *righteous* bandit. Stealing from the rich and what? Giving it back to the poor, or do you sell it for a nice profit?"

Dale's arms ached from being raised too long, fingers itching to reach for one of his weapons, but he knew Castle would pull the trigger before he moved a muscle.

"And are ya tryin' to start a war with all this? Why else would ya be makin' magic guns?"

"I'm a businessman. All I do is provide goods that people need. What they do with them is beyond my control."

"A real convenient excuse. Except how many people have ya hurt to create yer 'goods'? How many families didja tear apart for the sake of 'innovation'?" His mother's emblem glinted along the cylinder of Castle's gun.

Castle cocked his head to the side. "You seem to have a personal stake in this."

The burning questions in Dale's mouth singed his tongue. He felt time trickling away, and the prone men moved their arms. *Runnin' out of time. If I'm gonna get answers out of Castle and get outta here, I need to do somethin' now. Kaliska said I was good at gettin' myself out of sticky situations, but every plan I'm comin' up with now ends with a bullet through my head.*

As he thought through grabbing the gun, Kaliska dropped from the hatch in the ceiling and came swinging from behind. Castle whirled around to block her fist, and Dale reached for the gun. He managed to grab hold of the man's wrist before Castle shoved him to the ground. Dale rolled away from the boot slamming down toward him, losing his hat. He forgot about one of the guards behind him and stumbled, Castle's kick catching him in the side. The blow knocked his breath out of his lungs.

Bloody Inferno! The rich man has quite the kick. Must be his fancy boots. Dale grimaced and got to his knees. He spotted the bandolier a few feet away. *If I can get that, maybe we'll have the upper hand.*

Kaliska came at Castle again with a hatchet, trying to land a blow. Castle stared at her masked face as he avoided another attack. "So, *you're* Talon. You're what I expected an outlaw to look like," he said and leveled the gun at her. "I'll enjoy ripping that mask off your face."

One of the guards got up off the floor and lunged for Kaliska.

"Watch out!" Dale shouted, forgetting about the bandolier.

Kaliska turned on her heel and knocked the man aside, sending him crashing into a crate of guns. She swung her hatchet around and caught Castle in the cheek. He cursed as blood streamed down his face from a deep gash, and he sprinted for the other boxcar.

Scrambling to his feet, Dale tackled him before he could jump out. Dale wrestled him to the floor, seeing the other guards stumbling up. The butt of Castle's gun struck Dale in the jaw and sent starbursts dancing across his eyes. He pinned Castle's arm to the ground and pushed his elbow against the man's neck.

"Tell me where Alya and Marcus Hartwell are!" Dale said, spitting out a bloody glob on the floor.

"Who?" Castle struggled in Dale's grip, his sweaty hair plastered to his forehead.

"My parents. They were taken fifteen years ago from Boulder Rush. I've been searchin' for 'em, and now I find my Mama's symbol plastered on yer weapons. Why?!"

"Parents?" The man blinked before his eyes widened. "Alya always talked about a son."

Dale's breath hitched, and his grip loosened. "Is she still alive? What about my pa?" he pressed. "Where are they?"

Castle's gaze flicked to something behind Dale. Kaliska let out an angry yell, and hands yanked Dale back. Something metallic clattered to the floor, the sound lost in Dale's roaring pulse. Kaliska fought in the grip of three guards, her mask speckled with blood. Dale's captors shoved him to the ground, and he found himself staring at Castle's dragonhide boots.

"I applaud you for getting this far. I respect you for that," Castle said, fixing his hair and staring down at Dale with a lazy look. "But you both have put my livelihood in danger, and I can't allow that. This is the end of the line for you two."

"Tell me if my parents are alive!" Dale shouted. "Didja take 'em?"

"Your mother's mind was brilliant, and when I heard about the ingenious inventions to channel a new form of magic she'd been working on, I knew I needed her skills. She refused to sell them, so I had to convince her to see the error of her choice. Alya was as tough as that metal arm of hers, but she eventually saw sense, and now look at what she and I have built together. This will allow the common man to have the power of a mageslinger—erase the divide between the powerful and the powerless. Magic in the hands of everyone."

"Was brilliant?" Does that mean…? A pit formed in Dale's stomach as splinters from the floor dug into his cheek.

A shadow fell across the Pass outside, followed by the roar of ripping metal and splintering. Misae's claws tore through the boxcar roof, and sunlight broke through the dust and wood raining down. The whole train car rocked on the tracks, knocking the guards off balance. The crates of weapons fell as the white dragon bared her teeth, crouching over the car.

"Bloody Inferno!" Castle said, eyes wide. "An ancient dragon… So this is Talon's dragon."

Dale broke free and drew his gun. He fired a bullet into the leg of the nearest guard, who fell screaming. The rest of Castle's men drew their weapons and fired at Misae. She growled as the bullets deflected off her scales, and the boxcar shuddered when she moved. Kaliska fought her captors, bringing one to his knees. Dale looked for Castle through the hazy chaos and spotted him in the far corner, hauling a small cannon from a broken box.

Runes glowed around the barrel, and the air became charged, making the hairs along Dale's neck prickle. Kaliska's shout was broken by the boom of cannon fire that left Dale's ears ringing. Misae moved out of the way right as a round coated in fire and ice punched a hole through the membrane of her left wing. Her pained bellow threatened to blow out Dale's eardrums. Blood rained down, and Kaliska cut down another man. Misae lumbered away, each step shaking the boxcar.

Dale's gaze darted around to the scattered weapons and the

magic script flickering with green light. The charged air moved along his skin like needles, and a cold fear burgeoned in his chest.

That weapon can take down Misae. And he has a whole train full of 'em, he thought, gripping his revolver tighter as he raised it at Castle. *We won't stand a chance...No one will...*

Castle stood with the small cannon aimed at Dale and Kaliska, bleeding from cuts on his face. The remaining guards shoved them to the middle of the boxcar. "I'll send your regards to your parents in Edin," Castle told him. "I always wondered what this weapon would do to a dragon. Soon, battles and wars will change. Everything will change."

"Wait? Are my parents still alive?" Dale rasped, latching onto the present tense in Castle's ominous statement.

Fiery anger broke through the haze clinging to Dale's mind, and Bean's presence slammed into him before the dragon crashed into the train car. Bean roared, and a small jet of flame burned the air, engulfing the boxcar door. The remaining guards were knocked back as the dragon's tail swung wildly around. Dale fell against the wall with Kaliska beside him. Bean's emotions burned with sulfuric rage as he barreled into the boxcar and tossed aside Castle's guards. The floorboards groaned and split beneath him.

He's finally sparked. Thought I'd have to wait another ten years to see it happen. Dale's pride quickly turning to fear as he remembered the weapon Castle still held. The charged tang of magic building in the air felt like being caught in an electrical storm. Castle struggled under the weight of the cannon with a crazed look plastered across his sweaty face.

"We have to leave. Now!" Kaliska shouted and grabbed his arm.

"What about McCree and Castle? And the rest of the weapons?"

"Leave them! Chosovi took McCree and is waiting with the eggs away from here. Neither Misae nor your dragon can take a direct hit from any of these weapons, and they're about to go off!"

Bean continued his rampage, head swiveling toward Castle. The man loaded another round into the cannon. Misae's blood was still slick on the floor of the boxcar, the glowing words cutting through the smoke. Part of Dale hesitated, caught between wanting to grab Castle and not lose his answers, and the primal need to escape imminent danger.

"Bean, get us outta there!" Dale shouted. The dragon looked back at him, the rage dying from his amber eyes. Red stained his snout, and he let out a whimper. "Who knew all it would take for ya to spark is for us to be in a life-threatenin' situation."

"Less joking, Hartwell, and more escaping!" Kaliska hissed from behind him and whistled for Misae.

The ancient white dragon's shadow fell over them as she roared. Bean whined and lumbered over to Dale. Dale hauled himself into the saddle while Kaliska climbed on behind him and gripped his sides. Bean leapt out of the boxcar and ran across the ground to gain enough momentum for takeoff. Misae circled overhead, her injured wing flapping awkwardly. Dale looked back at the train as Castle appeared in the middle of the smoldering boxcar. The inside of the cannon barrel glowed, and Dale saw their end growing closer.

Without thinking, Dale raised his revolver and fired. Time moved as slow as molasses as the bullet flew and went down the cannon's barrel. A screeching whine cut the air before blinding light, and an explosion enveloped Castle and the boxcar. Bean leapt into the air as the blast rippled through the Pass, knocking him off course. Dale slammed against Bean's neck, the saddle horn digging into his stomach as Kaliska's weight was thrown against his back. Heat burned his skin, and smoke rose from the train like a dark hand grasping for the sky.

Bean crash landed on one of the rocky towers, talons digging into the rocks to stop himself. Dale blinked, staring at the wreckage of the train as it toppled off the tracks. The remaining terror bird riders and guards who had made it off the train were either thrown back by the blast or scattered to avoid the flaming debris raining down. No sign of Castle remained, and the last of his answers went up in flames. Dale's pulse thundered through him, his knuckles white around the reins.

"Guess I really won't be gettin' those gold scales now..." Dale muttered, and Bean launched into the sky. *Or any answers from him...*

Chapter 12

Into the Sunset

Dale leaned back in his saddle, the train smoldering in the distance against the sunset breaking through clouds. His body ached, and sweat stung the shrapnel cuts along his skin. Bean sat hunched on the clifftop overlooking the Viper's Pass. The acrid smell of dragonfire and burned oil still stung Dale's nose. The stragglers below moved about the wreckage like ants, their dragons and terror birds grounded a safe distance away. Dale turned over the last of Castle's words like he did his pendant until they were ingrained in his mind. Despite the exhaustion and ringing in his ears, the flicker of hope burned a little brighter.

Edin. I always wanted to go to the Steel City, Dale thought. *What'll happen to my parents now that Castle's dead? If his company collapses, they might be free to leave. Or was he lyin' about 'em bein' there?*

He glanced at Kaliska as she checked the eggs attached to Misae's saddle while Chosovi, the short-haired conductor, checked the weapon crates. The sky was orange and red, turning the dragon's white scales fiery. Fresh red marks from the enemy dragons marred Misae's body, and the hole in her wing from the canon blast had stopped bleeding. McCree's unconscious form was bound and gagged between two of Misae's spine ridges behind the saddle. Chosovi had deposited him on the ridge before the train blew and helped Kaliska secure the cargo.

"How do you feel about completing your first train heist?"

Kaliska asked, stopping to look at him. Soot still smudged her cheeks and forehead.

Dale blinked. "Are ya makin' a joke or sincerely askin' me?" She didn't reply. "So far train heists seem to end in explosions, which I can't say I'm partial to."

He patted Bean's side as the dragon spat out a burst of fire onto the ground, testing out his new abilities like a child with a new toy. All traces of his anger were gone as relief and wonderment took their place.

"I dunno how to describe it, but this all feels...unfinished. Like we worked so hard to find Castle, only to have him die suddenly. I feel almost cheated, ya know?"

Kaliska stopped and sighed. "I would have preferred him alive, but he played with something he shouldn't have, and he suffered the consequences. Sometimes this is how these things go. Some questions go unanswered and the things you work hard for don't always work out the way you want them. But I have more proof about what he's been doing than yesterday."

"I helped him along by shootin' the canon." *I've never caused a man to blow up before.* He grimaced. The bright explosion still burned behind his eyelids when he blinked.

"It saved us. It was a hard choice to make."

"What about ya, Kaliska? What are ya gonna do now?" Dale asked.

Her voice was quiet. "Castle may be gone, but there will be more men like him. And some have his weapons. His death will have ripple effects, and someone else is bound to continue what he started. No doubt the Alamedian military will investigate his death; I'm sure he had many of them in his pocket already. I'll take the weapons and the rest of my proof to the Council again and hope they can send a strong plea to the other Alluvialian cities."

Dale glanced at the white dragon. "No rest for ya, it seems." *Maybe I'll take Bill up on his offer to track down those gangs who have some of Castle's weapons.* "Are ya worried that they'll blame ya for the train explosion in Marrowville and Castle's death?"

"They could, but I think this will show them that oil magic is returning and could pose a bigger threat to everyone. I intend to seek restorations for the civilian lives lost in Marrowville. They had no idea what was on that train and suffered because of it."

"The sheriff of Marrowville is a good man. I could put in a good word for ya. Maybe with Castle's death, the bounty will be retracted."

"Sky Mother only knows. I'm sure there will be those foolish enough to try and come after me still."

Dale's gaze shifted to the white dragon. "Will Misae be alright?"

"The blast didn't tear any of the finger bones, just the membrane. It'll heal," Kaliska replied. She nodded to Chosovi once the netting holding the eggs together was secured. The other Alluvialian woman climbed into the saddle, wiping her hands off on her soot-streaked overalls. Trails of sweat streaked the black residue coating her face.

"Are you going to head to Edin now?"

"Yeah. If Castle's words are to be trusted, that's where my parents are. Figured this is where we part ways," Dale said.

"You could always come back to the village to heal up and rest before you set out."

"If I didn't know any better, I'd have thought ya genuinely wanted me to stay. Are ya catchin' feelin's for me?" Kaliska rolled her eyes. "It'll look cooler if I fly off into the sunset battered and beat up."

She pulled a pouch out of her saddlebags and threw it at him. He caught it, the weight hitting his chest like a light punch. The familiar clink of coins told him what was inside before he undid the strings. Gold scales glinted at him in the fading sunlight, and he let out a low whistle.

"Thought ya couldn't just hand out money that belonged to yer Council," he said.

"This was part of the stash Castle brought with him. It's not as much as my bounty was, but hopefully, it'll suffice."

"What's this other thing?" Dale asked and pulled out a brown, oblong shape the length of his finger.

"It's a messenger moth cocoon. If you need to get in touch with me, open it and whisper your message to the moth before it emerges. It'll find me. And you're not obligated to help me, but if you do find your parents and Castle's secret facility, I'd like to know."

"I s'pose I could let ya know what I find. Seems only fair. Don't worry, I won't tell anyone about ya or yer dragon."

She reached behind her and held up a brown wide-brimmed hat. "Don't think McCree needs this anymore. Try not to lose this one."

Putting the cocoon back in the pouch, Dale grinned and took the hat, placing it on his head. "This and the information are more than enough payment. I might be able to getcha some aurochs steaks, Bean. Or would you like some chili instead?" He patted the dragon's head and slipped the pouch into his saddle-bag. Bean wiggled, tail thumping against the ground.

"If you find your parents, you'll all be welcome in Chochmingwa. The Council will want to know all they can about the oil magic weapons, and they'll offer your parents protection should they need it."

Dale sat up. "Yer people would do that even though my mama helped design these weapons?"

"They were taken against their will. That's no fault of theirs."

"I'm sure my mama would love to see the village and the magic ya've been usin'. Pa would enjoy the different dragons, especially Misae."

"Until our paths cross again," Kaliska replied. "May the Sky Mother give you favorable winds."

Misae lowered her head toward Dale, his beat-up face reflected in her blue irises. *May the Winds grant you favor, Dale Hartwell,* she said. The rumbling pressure was more bearable in his head, leaving behind a soothing touch.

"Still not gonna get used to that." Dale tipped his hat to her. "See ya 'round then."

She nodded, lips curled upward in the faintest shadow of a smile. Putting on his goggles, Dale dug his heels into Bean's side, and the dragon launched off the cliff. His wings beat the air as they climbed skyward, circling above Kaliska and Misae once before melting into the horizon.

Mama, Pa, I'm comin' to find ya. Won't be much longer now.

Acknowledgments

Dear reader, thank you so much for picking up this novella and making it to the end! I remember when I had the idea for a cowboys and dragons story in 2019. It was mostly just vibes, and I wasn't sure where the story was going to go. For years, it was just called "Yeehaw Dragons" because I didn't have a good name for it until 2024. This story has grown from an idea about a cowboy and his dragon to the first installment to a fantasy Western series. Mostly, it was just a fun story to write because cowboys and dragons. What's not to love? Still, it's always nerve-wracking to jump into a new, unfamiliar genre and not knowing how the story will turn out.

I'm so thankful for my writing group (Sara, Tori, Shannan, Conner, and Kelsey) for looking at the rough draft of this story and giving me the feedback needed to make this better (and for loving Bean). I'm so blessed to have a group I can trust my work with. Also, another thank you to Tori Tecken, Jim, Cal, Emmy, Amber, and Claire for providing additional feedback. Everyone who looked at this story in the early stages played such an important role in shaping it into what it is today. I truly can't say thank you enough to all the readers who have picked up my works over the years. It means so much.

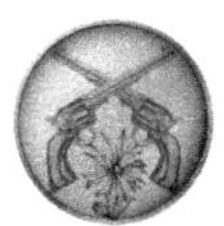

Books By K.E.Andrews

Let the Hurt Girl Speak

The Assassin of Grins and Secrets

Sonder and Morii

Let the Hurt Girl Heal

Seasons Unceasing: A Worldsmyths Anthology

Priestess of Moonlight

Hills of Heather and Bone

Under the Couch

Through the Valley: Devotionals for When You're in Life's Valleys

Connect With Me

Instagram: @k.e.andrews

Website: www.keandrews.org

Goodreads: K.E.Andrews

Facebook: @k.e.andrewsnovels

Twitter (X): @KEAndrews95

Don't forget to leave a review. You can also sign up for my newsletter to learn more about new projects, upcoming books, and more.

About the Author

K.E.Andrews has always been an avid reader, which sparked her passion for writing at an early age. Her love of traveling has taken her to different places around the world, reminding her that there are always more stories to tell. She is often found at her desk, attempting to write, binging Netflix, or trying to complete a craft project. She currently lives in Powder Springs, Georgia.